Stories of Surprise and Wonder

STORIES OF SURPRISE AND WONDER

ROBERT R. POTTER

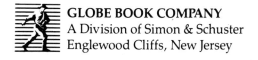

GLOBE BOOK COMPANY
A Division of Simon & Schuster
Englewood Cliffs, New Jersey

Cover Art: *The False Mirror,* René Magritte, 1928. Oil on canvas, 2 $^1/_4$" × 31 $^7/_8$". Collection, The Museum of Modern Art, New York.

Cover Design: Marek Antoniak

Illustrations by Karin Kretschmann

Photograph on page viii courtesy of Ontario Science Centre

Acknowledgments for previously published material appear on page 182 of this book.

ISBN: 0-83590-201-3

Printed in the United States of America.
10   9   8   7   6   5   4   3   2

Globe Book Company
A Division of Simon & Schuster
Englewood Cliffs, New Jersey

About the Author

ROBERT R. POTTER received his B.S. from the Columbia University School of General Studies and his M.A. and Ed.D. from Teachers College, Columbia University.

Dr. Potter has been a teacher of English in the New York City School System, a research associate for Project English at Hunter College, and a teacher of English at the Litchfield (Conn.) High School. He has held a professorship at the State University of New York and now teaches at the University of Connecticut's Torrington branch.

Dr. Potter is author of Globe's *Beyond Time and Space, Tales of Mystery and the Unknown, Myths and Folktales Around the World, The Reading Road to Writing, A Better Reading Workshop, Making Sense, Writing Sense, Writing a Research Paper, Language Workshop* and the consulting editor of *American Folklore and Legends* and the *Pathways to the World of English* series.

Contents

Bolts from the Blue

Spooks and Spirits

Shock Waves

Surprise and Wonder

Surprises are always new. They have to be. If we know about them beforehand, they aren't surprises.

Yet some surprises have been around for many years. Look at the picture below. It's been surprising people since 1846. Why? Just turn this page upside down.

See what we mean? The surprise was there waiting, all along.

Most days, as we know, hold few surprises. We live from minute to minute, from hour to hour. One day is just like the next. What we expect to happen does happen. And then suddenly—BANG! Our nice, neat world flips upside down. We gasp. We blink. We realize something we never knew before. It's as if a bolt of lightning hit us from out of a clear, blue sky.

The same thing can happen in our reading. In many books, of course, one story is just like the next. What we expect to happen *does* happen. But this book is different. A surprise lies waiting around every corner. And often, the stories bring with them a sense of wonder. New ideas sweep across our minds. We learn something that really matters.

Stories of Surprise and Wonder has three sections. The first is "Bolts from the Blue." It contains the kind of story we've been talking about. First we're surprised, and then we're forced to think. The second is "Spooks and Spirits." These stories also hold surprises—but something new has been added. We'll meet several grizzly ghosts and a few friendly phantoms. "Shock Waves" is the last section. Read these stories in a well-lit room. Sit up straight. Take a firm grip on the book. Breathe deeply, and expect the worst. It's guaranteed to happen.

BOLTS FROM THE BLUE

All that we see or seem
is but a dream within a
dream.

Edgar Allan Poe

The Eye Catcher

Frederick Laing

This book contains some tales that may make your teeth chatter. But let's start mildly. Let's start with a story about the nature of fear.

"The Eye Catcher" is a story about a girl named Genevieve. As you'll see, she's frightened of many things. At times, she's frightened of her mother's opinions. At other times, she's frightened of boys. And most of all, she's frightened of herself.

This is truly a story of surprise and wonder. It will make you think about the things we should all fear—and the things we shouldn't.

Vocabulary Preview

CONQUEST (KON kwest) something won, overcome, or conquered
  • Mary's latest *conquest* was climbing Mt. Washington.

CONSCIOUS (KON shus) aware, knowing; alert
  • Mandy was very *conscious* of the big bandage on her forehead.

FEDORA (fi DOR uh) a soft felt hat
  • The President waved his black *fedora* at the crowd.

FLATTERER (FLAT ur ur) a person who flatters, or says nice things, in order to please
  • A *flatterer* will say almost anything to please a teacher.

PROFILE (PRO file) the face as seen from the side
  • The photographer took both a *profile* and a full-face picture of the young woman.

WISTFULLY (WIST ful ee) in a sad, wishful manner
  • Matt looked *wistfully* at the motorcycle he couldn't buy.

HER REASON FOR SHOPPING IN WALLER'S

was not at all romantic. Her mother had told her to buy a rain hat. Something sensible, she'd said. Now she wandered through the department store. She looked sadly at the things she couldn't afford. She glanced wistfully at things she wouldn't be allowed to wear. That bikini swim suit, for instance. Renee Weston had one like it. . . .

Renee Weston, yes. . . . The girl Bert Howland was taking to the dance this Saturday. This very night! And as for herself, who had asked her? Why, nobody. For who was going to ask *her?* Who was going to ask quiet Genevieve Smith?

She was walking along the aisles. Her head hung down. And her heart, to judge by the way she felt, dragged on the floor behind her. It was the hair ribbons that stopped her cold. Then she saw the sign:

"EYE CATCHERS," it said.

And around the sign was a big selection of bow ribbons. They were new, happy, bright! She had never seen anything like them. Every color of the rainbow, it said. Pick a color to suit your personality.

She stood there a moment with her head down. Would her mother let her wear one? No, she decided. Not a bow that big and showy even if she had the nerve, which she hadn't. Those eye catchers, they were the kind. . . .

The kind Renee Weston would wear! She stood there thinking. Suddenly the clerk broke into her thoughts. "This would be a nice one for you, dearie."

5

"Oh, no, I'm afraid ... " she replied. "I'm afraid I couldn't wear anything like that." But at the same time she reached out for the green ribbon.

The clerk looked surprised. "With that lovely copper-colored hair? And those lovely eyes? Why, honey, you could wear anything."

Maybe it was only a sales talk. But the ribbon was attached to a comb. And she didn't need much urging. She fastened it into her hair.

"No, a little farther front," the clerk said. "There's one thing you have to remember, honey. If you're going to wear a crazy thing like that, wear it like nobody had a better right than you. In this world, you gotta hold your head up." She looked at the position of the ribbon. "That's better. Why, you look really ... exciting."

She looked in the mirror. Sure enough, the green color of the ribbon, and the hint of red in her hair, with the green of her eyes. . . .

"I'll take it," she said. She was a little surprised at the note of decision in her voice.

"Now, you might want another for formal wear," the clerk said. "One like this, for instance. If you were going to a party or a dance. . . ."

That was the last thing she wanted to think about. She paid for the ribbon in a hurry. She started to get out of there so fast that she bumped smack into a big woman with a lot of packages. She almost got knocked silly.

As she neared the door, a funny old man was beside her, staring at her. A man with black eyes. She noticed a droopy gray mustache under a green fedora hat. You could tell from the eyes that he was smiling under the gray mustache. Smiling and looking at the eye catcher. Or *was* it a smile?

Well, it was a conquest, she thought. A conquest, even

6

if it wasn't much. She gave him a glance. Just a little passing look, but. . . .

But the next moment a shiver of fright went through her. The silly old thing was actually following her! That eye catcher couldn't. . . . But this was really awful! She started to look around. Then she heard him say, "Hey, keedo!"

What should she do? She speeded up. Half a block away, she looked behind her. The man was still coming, faster now. Suddenly she found herself running. She ran like a rabbit. She didn't stop till she was over a block down the street.

Then suddenly she found herself in front of Carson's drugstore. She knew for sure it was where she'd been running to from the start. Some of her girl friends might be there. Bert Howland might even be there. It was where he often hung around Saturday afternoon. He talked with his friends or played the pinball machine.

She stopped just a moment before she entered. Then she took a deep breath.

Bert was there all right. He was sitting at the lunch counter. He was hunched over a cup of coffee, not drinking it, just looking ahead. The minute she saw him, she thought, "Renee turned him down. She's going to the dance with someone else."

She sat down at the other corner of the counter facing his profile. Harry, smiling in his white apron, came over to take her order.

"Bring me a Coke," she said.

Harry turned to get her order. Now she could see Bert again, out of the side of her eyelashes. He had turned and was staring at her.

She sat up straight, holding her head high. She was conscious, very conscious, of that green eye catcher.

7

After a while he said, "Hi, Genevieve."

She turned, doing a neat little job of looking surprised. "Why, Bert Howland," she said. "How long have you been sitting here?"

"All my life," he said. "Just waiting for you."

It was only a line. But ordinarily it would have left her stuttering. She wanted to reach up and touch her hair. She wanted to feel the eye catcher to give her more confidence. It was a battle to keep her hands on the counter.

"Flatterer!" she said.

And a moment later, he was sitting on the stool beside her. He was looking at her in the same way. It was as if he'd just noticed that she was alive.

"Wearing your hair a different way?" he asked. "There's *some* difference, isn't there?"

She reached for her Coke and took a gulp. "Do you usually notice things like that?" she asked.

"No," he said. "I guess it's just the way you're holding your head up. Like you thought I ought to notice something."

She felt a slight blush. Her cheeks and the tips of her ears tingled. "Is that meant as a crack?"

"Maybe," he said, grinning. "And maybe not. Maybe I sort of like to see you hold your head like that."

It was about ten minutes later that the impossible happened. He said, "You know, they're having a big dance at the club tonight."

And soon he actually came across with it, the invitation and everything. It was all she could do to say "Yeah, I guess so" and smile.

They left the drugstore a little later. He offered to walk home with her. But suddenly she remembered that formal eye catcher, the one you wore to a party or a dance. She couldn't wear the green one she had on. She would need one to match her new dress. And so she told him that she simply had to get to Waller's before it closed.

She got there just as the doors were being shut. A man tried to keep her out. But she brushed past him and dashed to the ribbon counter.

She looked for the blue-and-gold one. Gone! If they didn't have another. . . .

The clerk smiled when she saw who it was. "I knew you'd be back."

"H . . . how?" she asked, out of breath.

The clerk reached under the counter. "I've been saving it for you." But the eye catcher she brought out was not the blue-and-gold one. It wasn't even formal at all. In fact, it was . . .

"That's like the one I just bought," she said, puzzled.

And then she was standing with her mouth open in wonder. Why, when the big woman had bumped into her. . . . The eye catcher must have been knocked off.

"It *is* the same one," the clerk explained.

And with that knowledge a lot of things began to flash through Genevieve's mind. But suddenly she began to smile. Then she couldn't stop smiling. She let her head lift easily. Only half of her listened to the clerk's story. It was a story about a man who had picked up the eye catcher and tried to give it back to her—a jolly old man in a green fedora hat.

Recall

1. Genevieve enters the department store to (a) waste some time (b) buy a rain hat (c) buy a hair ornament

2. As the man with the mustache follows her down the street, Genevieve feels (a) proud (b) interested in the man (c) frightened
3. Genevieve is mistaken in thinking that she (a) is wearing the eye catcher in the drugstore (b) might go to the dance with Bert (c) has learned something about herself
4. The eye catcher that is saved by the clerk for Genevieve is (a) blue and gold (b) blue and green (c) green
5. At the end of the story, we know that the old man was (a) a danger to all women (b) an employee of the store (c) no harm at all

Infer

6. Genevieve's attitude toward Renee Weston can best be described by the word (a) *hate* (b) *envy* (c) *love*
7. "It was about ten minutes later that the impossible happened." A word in this sentence that does not really mean what it says is (a) *minutes* (b) *impossible* (c) *happened*
8. From the beginning of the story to the end, Genevieve passes from (a) uneasiness to confidence (b) confidence to foolish wildness (c) knowledge to ignorance
9. In the last paragraph we read that "a lot of things began to flash through Genevieve's mind." One of these things was probably that (a) she will surely marry Bert someday (b) Bert likes things such as eye catchers (c) Bert likes her for herself
10. Which sentence best expresses the meaning of the story? (a) The way you dress makes all the difference. (b) Ignore old people who frighten you. (c) Be proud of what you are.

Vocabulary Review

1. At the end of the story, Bert and Genevieve regard each other as (a) *flatterers* (b) *conquests* (c) *profiles*
2. The person in the story who cannot possibly be regarded as a *flatterer* is (a) Genevieve (b) Bert (c) the clerk
3. The green *fedora* mentioned in the story was a (a) frightened old man (b) felt hat (c) hair bow
4. If Bert looked *wistfully* across the counter at Genevieve, he probably looked as if he (a) wished he knew her better (b) had given up all hope (c) felt sorry for her
5. A *profile* of Bert's face would probably show (a) one ear (b) two ears (c) just the center of the face
6. As Genevieve sat at the counter, she was *conscious* of her posture. In other words, she was (a) careless of it (b) worried about it (c) very aware of it

Critical Thinking

1. The title of the story has a double meaning. Of course, "eye catcher" refers to the hair bow. But what else might it mean? Explain.
2. Who gives Genevieve the best advice in the story? What is that advice, in one sentence? (Look back if you wish.) Do you think that advice would be good for all people you know? A few people? Most people? Explain.

11

3. Like many stories in this book, "The Eye Catcher" has a surprise ending. Did you like the ending? Or did you feel tricked? Did you guess the ending? If so, explain how you figured it out.

4. "Pick a color to suit your personality." In your opinion, what does Genevieve's first selection of green indicate? What color would you pick for her at the end of the story? List at least five colors, and next to them describe the types of personalities you think they might stand for.

The Bet

Anton Chekhov

*Some stories in this book contain surprises that shock
us. Others contain wonders that make us think. But
some stories contain both surprise and wonder.
Anton Chekhov's "The Bet" is one of these tales.*

   *Anton Chekhov was a Russian. He lived about
a hundred years ago. He wrote about the people he
knew in the Russia of long ago. But in another
sense, he wrote about all people everywhere. Many of
his ideas will never die. That's why he's now called
a "classic" writer.*

Vocabulary Preview

CAPITAL (KAP uh tul) having to do with death
- The term *capital punishment* means "punishment by death."

CONFINEMENT (kon FINE ment) the holding of someone, as in prison; imprisonment
- After a year's *confinement,* the prisoner was glad to be free again.

NOVEL (NOV ul) a book-length story
- Dad gets a mystery *novel* from the library every week.

ROUBLE (ROO bul) a piece of Russian money
- We save our dollars; the Russians save their *roubles.*

RUMORS (ROO murs) stories that may be untrue; pieces of gossip
- I heard *rumors* that our principal was quitting.

SOLITARY (SOL uh ter ee) existing without others; alone
- In some prisons, people are kept in *solitary* confinement.

TARNISH (TAR nish) to darken; to ruin a reputation
- Let our school's good name never be *tarnished* by others!

CAPITAL PUNISHMENT!" CRIED SOMEONE in the room. "Why, it's something left over from the dim, dark ages. It isn't modern! It isn't *right!*"

A group of clever successful people had gathered at the home of a young banker. The talk had somehow gotten around to the death penalty. Now the host had a lively argument on his hands.

"I'm sorry, but I can't agree with you," the banker stated. "Of course, I've never suffered the death penalty myself. Neither have I ever suffered solitary confinement. But just think about it! Imagine yourself in prison for life, alone, totally alone. Putting a man to death seems a thousand times better than that. Now tell me, which is more kind? To end your life in one quick minute? Or to draw out your suffering year after wasted year—"

"No! No! They are both horrible," put in one of the guests. "But to take away a life—? Who should take life but the Lord? Why should the government have this power? Can the government restore life? No. The government is not God. It has no right to take human life."

Now it was a young lawyer's turn. "No doubt you are right," he said. He seemed to be thinking the matter over, deeply. "Both punishments are perhaps without justice. But as for me, I know which I would choose. *Any* kind of life is better than death. Even solitary confinement would be better than—"

"Nonsense!"

"It is so!"

"No!"

"Yes!"

Half a dozen voices all sounded at once. The host, a banker, banged on the table for silence. He stood looking at the lawyer.

15

"What you say is not true," stated the banker. "It is a stupid thing to say. Two million roubles! I'll bet you two million roubles that you can't stand solitary confinement. A lifetime? Bah! Just five years. Two million roubles for five of your years!"

"Do you mean that?" asked the lawyer.

"Two million roubles!"

"I accept your bet," said the lawyer simply. "And I'll give you more years—fifteen years. I will stay in solitary confinement for fifteen years. Then you will give me two million roubles."

"Fifteen! Fifteen!" cried the banker. He was now wildly excited, as though he had already won the bet. "I accept. The people here are our witnesses. I stake two million roubles. You stake fifteen years of your freedom."

It was a cruel, stubborn, senseless bet. Many of the guests tried to get them to forget it. But the banker would not forget. He had recently made a lot of money in a business deal. To him, two million roubles was nothing! All through dinner, he kept talking about the bet. Worse than that, he kept teasing the young lawyer.

"Well now, my friend," he would call across the table. "Have you changed your mind yet? Two million is nothing to me. But three or four years of your life! That's something to think about. That's right—I said three or four years. You'll never stick it out longer than that, I can tell you. And they'll just be wasted years. Not one penny do I give you if you leave early. Why, think of it, my friend! My jail will have no bars, no locks. You'll be able to walk out of it any minute. That thought will be like a poison to you. So you *will* walk out; I know that. Sooner or later, you'll walk out."

In a few days the "prison" was ready. It was in an old building in back of the banker's house. For fifteen years the lawyer was not to pass through its door. For fifteen years he was not to see any other human being. He was not to hear a human voice. He was not to receive letters or newspapers. Musical instruments, however, were to be permitted. So were books. So were wine and tobacco. Some other things he could order. He had only to pass his order note through a window. A guard would bring anything allowed.

Thus, the smallest details of the bet were discussed and settled. At twelve noon on November 14, 1870, the prison term began. It was to last until twelve noon on November 14, 1885. The lawyer must make no attempt to break the rules agreed upon. The slightest attempt would mean loss of the money.

The lawyer's first year was one of suffering. He grew bored. Even the piano did not cheer him. Wine he did not ask for, nor tobacco. Short, easy novels were his only reading; he devoured them by the dozen. During the second year, the sound of the piano, once heard often, stopped completely. Great books of the world's literature became his only reading.

By the fifth year, the piano was heard again. One day he asked for wine. Was he doing better? Perhaps. But guards who peered into his room saw him banging the walls, kicking things. He often threw himself on the bed, to cry for hours. He seemed completely bored and hopeless. These moods would be followed by fits of anger. He would write for hours at his desk. Then, in a blind rage, he would tear his work into thousands of pieces.

But things grew better in the years that followed. He read the great books of history. He studied languages. He studied science. In just a few years he read over 600 difficult books. Genius seemed to have flared up in the prisoner. It burned steadily in him—a genius for study, knowledge, and thought.

More than ten years had now passed. One day he asked for the Bible. It was sent to him. And for a whole year —hour after hour, day after day—he studied it. Then came other books on religion. All kinds of literature. Medicine. More science. More art. He seemed surrounded by a sea of words.

At last the end grew near. Now it was twelve midnight, the night before the prisoner's term would end. The banker walked back and forth in his room. "I shall be without a penny tomorrow," he told himself. "To pay off the bet, I must come up with two million roubles. What will be left? Nothing. I shall be ruined."

It was indeed true. The fifteen years had not been kind to the banker. His business deals had gone sour. His little worries had become horrible fears.

"A bet, was it?" he asked himself. "It was *not* a bet! It was a suicide plan—for me. That man is going to destroy me. Only forty years old! Why, he will take my money and laugh in my face.

"No! No! He may not laugh. He may say, 'I owe it all to you, my friend. Here, take some of my money. Let me help you!' Oh, such shame!" To the banker, this thought was worse than the idea of being poor.

"This is too much to bear," the banker went on. "Too much for anyone. Ruin and shame! I must escape, even if he has to die—*even if he has to die!*"

The banker stopped still, the last words ringing in his ears. Long he stood there. As the clock struck three, noisy leaves argued with the night wind. A cold rain swept against the dark windows.... And soon, outside, the rain beat against the banker's bare head. Quickly he reached the house of the prisoner. It stood quietly under the rain.

"Ivan! Ivan!" called the banker. The guard did not answer.

"Must be sleeping," the banker told himself. "Good, good. Now is the time! If only I have the courage, Ivan will get the blame."

There was no one at the door. It opened without a sound. The prisoner's room was lit by the light of a dying lamp. And there sat the prisoner at his desk. He looked asleep. The banker tapped on the door frame. No sign from the other. He looked like a skinny skeleton. Long, matted hair fell on his shoulders. His cheeks were sunken. His skin was yellow with the color of the earth—the earth from which it had come, and to which it would soon return. The prisoner's right hand rested on a sheet of paper in front of him. What a hand! A deathly hand. A deathly hand with a skeleton finger pointing at the prisoner's last words.

"Easy now, easy," the banker told himself. "He's not a strong man. I can smother him with a pillow. There will be no fight, no noise, no bloody wound. Nothing that would look like a murder."

Softly, the banker crept forward. His eyes dropped to the paper. Very gently, he moved the pointing finger that hid some of the words:

Tomorrow, at noon, I am to have my freedom. But what a joke it is to me now! Why should I want that kind of freedom? I now know that it is worth nothing. For years I have known your world better than you who lived in it. I have traveled everywhere. I have done everything. I have seen the sun over Mount Blanc, and the sunset staining sky and ocean with purple. Spirits have spoken to me of God. Words have brought me wonder and wisdom.

And what have I learned? That your world is worthless. That the things you value are false and empty. Your history, your so-called wisdom, your money-hungry race through life—to me these are no more than the story of mice that die under your floors. The only true freedom is freedom of the mind. To enjoy beauty! To learn! To think! To grow wise! You have exchanged the worth of heaven for the stuff of the earth. Tomorrow I should receive two million roubles. But they are without value. I shall gladly give them up. Five hours before noon I shall leave my prison. I shall break the rules, and lose the bet. Nothing will be owing to me.

For a moment the banker could hardly believe his eyes. His face grew red as he skimmed the letter again. Yes, it was true! He bent over and kissed the head of the strange man in front of him.

All that night, the banker lay crying tears of guilt and joy. In the morning, the guard came to tell him that the prisoner's cell was empty. The banker hurried to see if this were true. It was, and the banker was happy to see that the note was still in place. Very carefully, he picked it up and made two neat folds. Back in his house, he locked the note in his safe. He had won the bet, hadn't he? And no rumors around town were going to tarnish his victory!

Recall

1. The idea for the bet first comes from (a) the lawyer (b) a group of guests at the party (c) the banker
2. Strangely, the person who increases the original five years to fifteen is the (a) lawyer (b) banker (c) judge

3. During his last ten years in prison, the lawyer passes from (a) faith to doubt (b) sanity to insanity (c) unhappiness to happiness
4. Toward the end of the story, the banker decides to (a) join the prisoner in a lifetime of study (b) accept his own ruin cheerfully (c) murder the prisoner
5. The person who wins the bet concerning the money is the (a) lawyer (b) banker (c) judge

Infer

6. At the end of the story, the happiest person is the (a) lawyer (b) banker (c) judge
7. "Short, easy novels were his only reading; he devoured them by the dozen." A word in this sentence that does not really mean what it says is (a) *novels* (b) *devoured* (c) *dozen*
8. At the end, the person most sensitive to what other people might think is the (a) lawyer (b) prison guard (c) banker
9. We can tell from the story that the author, Anton Chekhov, had (a) once served a long prison term (b) long been against the death penalty (c) thought about the meaning of life
10. Which sentence best expresses the main idea of the story? (a) "Who should take life but the Lord?" (b) "He seemed surrounded by a sea of words." (c) "The only true freedom is freedom of the mind."

Vocabulary Review

Write on your paper the word in *italics* that belongs in each blank on page 22.

capital	novel	rumor	tarnish
confinement	rouble	solitary	

1. A prisoner that is kept alone in a cell is said to be in
_____ _____.

2. The _____ that Yvonne and Juan are engaged is untrue.

3. A _____ crime is one you can be killed for committing.

4. Anton Chekhov wrote many plays and short stories, but not a single _____.

5. That old Russian _____ will _____ unless you polish it regularly.

Critical Thinking

1. Explain in your own words what happened to the lawyer during his fifteen years in prison. Stress the latter part of the prison term. Pay particular attention to the letter the prisoner writes.

2. The banker is an interesting character. Explain how the following words apply to him at different times in the story: *pride, shame, guilt, joy.*

3. This story, which happens in nineteenth-century Russia, starts with a discussion of capital punishment. The argument is still going on today. Where do you stand on these questions? Is it fairer to kill a convicted murderer than to put him or her in jail for life? Is it wrong for the government to kill *anyone,* no matter how serious the crime? Explain your thinking.

4. Suppose someone made *you* this offer: five years in solitary confinement for two million dollars. Would you even consider it? Think twice! Explain the advantages and disadvantages of each decision.

A Tale of Terror

Paul Louis Courier

*Just imagine this tale . . . you're traveling through
a strange land. The people there, you believe, hate
people from your country. One day you get lost.
After dark, you knock at the door of a house. You're
taken in, fed, and offered a bed. But you can't sleep.
You can't help worrying. Then, toward morning, you
hear voices. You hear people planning your own
death! A tale of terror? Yes, by Paul Louis Courier,
a Frenchman who lived and wrote about 200 years
ago.*

Vocabulary Preview

ARSENAL (AR suh nul) a place where guns, bullets, etc. are stored
  • The soldiers went to the *arsenal* for more ammunition.

CALABRIA (kuh LAY bree uh) a region in southwest Italy
  • Tony's great-grandmother came from *Calabria*.

CAPON (KAY pon) a kind of chicken raised for eating
  • A large *capon* is the size of a small turkey.

LOFT (LAWFT) an attic; a shallow place under a roof
  • The cabin had a small *loft* where people slept.

PROVISIONS (pro VIZH unz) food supplies
  • The campers' *provisions* included dried meat, potatoes, and fruit.

I WAS ONCE TRAVELING IN CALABRIA. IT IS a land of wicked people I believe they hate everyone, particularly French people like myself. The reason would take too long to tell you. It is enough to say that they mortally hate us. French people get on very badly when they fall into the hands of Calabrians.

I had a young man for a companion. In those mountains the roads are steep. Our horses got on with much difficulty. My companion went first. A path that seemed to him shorter led us astray. It was my fault. Should I have trusted a head only twenty years old?

While daylight lasted, we tried to find our way through the wood. But the more we tried, the more lost we became. It was pitch dark when we came to a very evil-looking house. We entered, not without fear. But what could we do?

We found a whole family of coal miners at the table. They asked us to join them. My young man did not wait to be asked twice. Soon we were eating and drinking. He, at least, was, for I was looking around at the place and the people. Pieces of dark, smoked meat hung here and there on the ceiling. Our hosts had quite the look of miners. But the house you would have taken for an arsenal. There were guns, pistols, swords, and knives of all kinds. Everything displeased me. And I saw very well that I displeased our hosts.

But my companion was quite one of the family. He laughed and talked with them. I should have foreseen his stupidity! He told them where we came from. He told them where we were going. He told them that we were Frenchmen! Just imagine! We were among our worst enemies. We

25

were alone, lost, and far from all human help. And then, to leave out nothing that might ruin us, he played the rich man. For their help, he offered to give them whatever they wished when we left.

Then he spoke of his bag. He begged them to help him care for it. He wanted it put at the head of his bed. He did not wish, he said, for any other pillow. Oh, youth, youth! You are to be pitied! One would have thought we carried the king's diamonds. In truth, I knew why he valued that bag. It wasn't the king's diamonds. It was his girlfriend's letters.

Supper over, they left us. Our hosts slept below, we in an upper room. A loft seven or eight feet high was to be our resting place. It was reached by a ladder. It was a kind of nest. You got into it by creeping under beams loaded with provisions for the year. My companion climbed up alone. Nearly asleep, he laid himself down with his head on the bag.

I decided to sit up. I made a good fire in a small stove and sat down beside it. There, not daring to sleep, I passed the night.

Toward morning, I began to be less fearful. The night was nearly over when I heard voices. Our host and his wife were talking and arguing below. I put my ear to the chimney. I clearly heard these words spoken by the husband:

"Well, let's see, must they both be killed?"

To which the wife replied, "Yes."

I heard no more. How shall I go on? I stood scarcely breathing. My body was cold as stone. You could hardly have known if I were alive or dead. Good heavens, when I think of it now! We two were almost without weapons. We were against a large family who had so many!

My companion was still dead with sleep. To call him, or make a noise, I dared not. To escape alone was impossible.

The window was not high. But outside were two large dogs howling like wolves.

At the end of a long quarter-hour, I heard someone on the stairs. I looked through the crack in the door. I saw the husband. A lamp was in one hand, and in the other one of the long knives. He came up, his wife after him. I was behind the door. He opened it. But before he came in, he put down the lamp, which his wife took. He then entered, barefoot. From the outside the woman said, "Softly, go softly." She spoke in a low voice, shading the lamp with her hand. When he got to the ladder, he started up. His knife was between his teeth. Getting up as high as the bed——— The poor young man lying with his throat bare——— With one hand he took his knife, and——— Oh! With the other—he seized a ham, which hung from the ceiling. He cut a slice from it. Then he left as he had come. The door was closed again. The lamp disappeared. I was left alone with my thoughts.

Soon the sun rose. The family came to awaken us, as we had asked. They brought us something to eat. It was a very good breakfast, I assure you. Two capons formed part of it. We must, said our hostess, eat one and take the other away. When I saw the capons, I understood the meaning of those terrible words: "Must they both be killed?" And I think I don't have to say now what they meant.

Recall

1. The two travelers entered the house because (a) the coal-mining family forced them in (b) it was night, and they were tired and hungry (c) the younger man was wounded

2. The narrator (the person who tells the story) feels quite sure they will be (a) treated well (b) made to work in the mines (c) harmed in some way
3. As the husband climbs the ladder, the narrator hides (a) in the loft (b) behind the door (c) under his bed
4. The big surprise in the story concerns the use made of a (a) knife (b) bag (c) lamp

Infer

5. The person in the story who is most mistaken is the (a) narrator (b) young traveling companion (c) husband
6. The narrator's attitude toward his young traveling companion is one of (a) deep trust and friendship (b) fierce hate (c) snobbish superiority
7. The narrator does not climb up to his bed because (a) his companion snores (b) he needs the warmth of a fire (c) he is too worried to sleep
8. "Must they both be killed?" The narrator *first* thinks that this question refers to (a) capons (b) the coal miners (c) himself and his companion
9. At the end of the story, the narrator knows that "must they both be killed?" referred to (a) capons (b) the coal miners (c) himself and his companion
10. The main idea of the story is that suspicious, frightened people often (a) are tempted to fight with others (b) put their own meanings into the words and actions of other people (c) have trouble sleeping

Vocabulary Review

1. In an *arsenal* you might expect to find (a) many cans of gasoline (b) rifles and bullets (c) food supplies
2. Instead of "food supplies" in the last question, which word might have been used? (a) *providers* (b) *proverbs* (c) *provisions*
3. A *Calabrian capon* might correctly be called a(n) (a) Italian chicken (b) chicken cooked with wine and cheese sauce (c) type of Italian apron
4. A *loft* is always reached by going (a) down (b) sideways (c) up

Critical Thinking

1. "A Tale of Terror" has a tricky ending. Did you see it coming? If so, you noticed the clues in the story. What are these clues?
2. Even today, many people are suspicious of foreigners. What is the author saying "between the lines" about such suspicions?
3. Suppose you had been along with the two travelers. Would you have behaved more like the narrator, or more like his companion? Explain.

4. " 'A Tale of Terror' is a well-told tale." Think of three details to support that statement. Consider the setting and the time of the story. Why does the author mention the "arsenal"? What does the use of the long dashes (———) on page 29 add to the story?

The Last Leaf

O. Henry

His real name was William Sidney Porter. He was born in North Carolina, in 1862. His early life was hardly promising—little schooling, odd jobs in a drugstore, on a ranch, and in a bank. In 1896 he was charged with stealing money while working in a bank in Austin, Texas. He served three years in jail.

There Porter's life took a surprising turn. While in jail he practiced writing short stories. He signed them "O. Henry." Soon he was a famous author. Today he is remembered as the master of the trick ending.

O. Henry's stories were written about seventy-five years ago. Some of them now seem old-fashioned. The "trick" endings may be easy to figure out. But not "The Last Leaf." It remains a masterpiece.

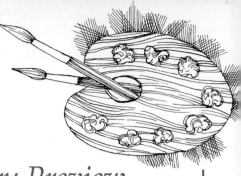

Vocabulary Preview

CANVAS (KAN vus) the piece of heavy cloth that an artist paints on
  • The painter set up a blank *canvas* and began work.

MASTERPIECE (MAS tur pees) the best work of a top artist or writer
  • O. Henry's best story should be called his *masterpiece.*

MODEL (MOD ul) a person who poses for an artist or photographer
  • Top fashion *models* earn $100 an hour.

PNEUMONIA (noo MONE ya) a serious disease of the lungs
  • Before modern drugs, *pneumonia* took many lives every winter.

STALKED (STAWKD) walked in a stiff, proud manner
  • The prisoner was found guilty, but she *stalked* out of the room like an innocent woman.

STUDIO (STOO dee oh) the workroom of an artist
  • A good *studio* has its windows on the north side for better light.

JUST WEST OF NEW YORK CITY'S WASH-
ington Square, the streets have run crazy. They make strange
angles and curves. One street crosses itself a time or two. A
poor artist once discovered that this was *just* the place to
live. Suppose a bill collector came. On streets like these, he
might suddenly meet himself coming back. Without a cent
having been paid on any of his bills!

So here, years ago, the art people came in great num-
bers. The area was—and still is—called Greenwich Village.
Young artists poured in from all over the country. They were
looking for north windows and low rents.

And here, Sue and Johnsy had their art studio. "Johnsy"
was a nickname for *Joanna.* They rented the top of a three-
story brick building. One was from Maine; the other from
California. The girls had met at an Eighth Street cafeteria.
Their tastes in art were the same. Their tastes in food were
the same. So the shared studio was a natural result.

That was in May. In November came a cold, unseen
stranger, whom the doctors called pneumonia. He stalked
about the city. With icy fingers, he touched one here, one
there. Over on the East Side, he walked boldly. Dozens, even
hundreds, died. But he had to walk slowly through the
crooked, narrow streets of Greenwich Village.

Mr. Pneumonia was hardly a kind old man. He was red
fisted and short of breath. And a young woman from California was hardly fair game for him. But Johnsy he touched.

33

Soon she lay, scarcely moving, on her bed. She grew even more ill. Day after day, she lay staring through the window. Outside the window was the blank wall of an old brick house.

One morning the busy doctor paid a visit. He looked at Johnsy. Then he invited Sue into the hallway by raising his shaggy, gray eyebrow.

"I could put her in the hospital," the doctor said. "But beds are scarce. And besides, she's just as well off here."

Sue nodded.

"She has one chance in—let us say, ten," the doctor went on. "And that chance is for her to want to live. You see, she's joined the crowd lining up for the funeral director. That kind of thing makes us doctors look silly. She's decided for herself that she's not going to get well. Has she anything on her mind?"

"She used to," Sue replied. "She—she wanted to paint the Bay of Naples someday."

"Paint? Bosh! Has she anything on her mind worth thinking about twice? A man, for instance?"

"A man?" said Sue. Doubt shaded her voice. "Is a man worth———? But no, doctor. Nothing of the kind."

"Well, it's the illness, then," said the doctor. "I will do all that I can do. But that girl is already counting the people at her funeral. When that happens, I subtract fifty percent from the powers of our medicines. You just get her to ask one question about something she really likes. Just one question. Then I'll give you a one-in-five chance for her."

The doctor left. Sue went into their workroom. She cried a napkin soggy with tears. Then she walked brightly into Johnsy's room. She carried her drawing board. She whistled a jazz tune.

Johnsy lay with her face toward the window. Was she asleep? Sue thought so. She stopped whistling. She sat down to work on her drawing. It was a picture for a magazine story.

For a while Sue worked on the figure of the hero, an Idaho cowboy. Then she heard a low sound. It was repeated. She went quickly to the bedside.

Johnsy's eyes were wide open. She was looking out the window. She was counting—counting backward.

"Twelve," she said. Then, a little later, "Eleven." Next came ten and nine. Finally she said, "Eight."

Sue was worried. She glanced out the window. What was there to count? There was only a bare, dreary yard to be seen. The yard, and the side of the brick house twenty feet away. An old, old ivy vine crawled up the brick wall. The cold breath of autumn had touched the vine. Its skeleton branches were almost bare.

"What is it, Johnsy?" asked Sue.

"Seven," said Johnsy. She spoke in almost a whisper. "They're falling faster now. Three days ago there were almost a hundred. It made my head ache to count them. But now it's easy. There goes another one. There are only six left now."

"Six *what*, Johnsy? Tell me!"

"Leaves. On the ivy vine. When the last one falls, I must go, too. I've known that for three days. Didn't the doctor tell you?"

"Oh, that's nonsense!" complained Sue. "What have those old ivy leaves to do with *you?* With your getting well? And you used to love that vine so. Don't be a goose. Why, your chances are good, Johnsy. The doctor told me just now —— Let's see exactly what he said—— He said the chances were ten to one! There's really no reason to worry, Johnsy. Try to take some soup now. And let Sue get back to her drawing. I've got to sell it to that magazine. Then we'll have money for—for pork chops!"

"You needn't get any pork chops for me," said Johnsy. She kept her eyes fixed out the window. "There goes another. No, I don't want any soup. The last one will fall before it gets dark. Then I'll go, too."

"Johnsy, dear!" exclaimed Sue. "Look, I want you to promise me something. Promise to keep your eyes closed. Don't look out the window till I'm done working. My drawings are due tomorrow. I need the light, or I'd pull the shade down."

"Couldn't you draw in the other room?" Johnsy's voice was cold.

"I'd rather be here by you," said Sue.

"Tell me when you're done," said Johnsy. She closed her eyes. Her face was white. She lay still as a fallen statue. "You see, I want to see that last leaf fall. I'm tired of waiting. I'm tired of thinking. I want to turn loose my hold on everything. Then I'll go sailing down, down. Just like one of those poor, tired leaves."

"Try to sleep," said Sue. "I must go see Behrman. He's to be my model for the older cowboy. I'll not be gone a minute. Try not to move till I come back."

Old Behrman was a painter. He lived downstairs, on the ground floor. He was past sixty. He was a failure in art. For forty years he had painted, without success. He'd been always about to paint a masterpiece. But he'd never yet begun it. Now he earned a little money by working as a model. He drank too much, and he still talked of his masterpiece. For the rest, he was a fierce little old man. He hated softness in anyone. He thought of himself as the protector of the two young artists in the studio above.

Sue found Behrman at home. His breath smelled strong. In one corner of his den was a blank canvas. It had been waiting there twenty-five years for the first line of his masterpiece. She told him of Johnsy's thoughts: "She's as light as a leaf herself. She might really float away. Her hold on the world gets weaker and weaker."

Old Behrman's red eyes went wet. He waved his arms and shouted.

"What!" he cried. "Is there people in the world with such foolishness? To die because a leaf drops off a vine? I have not heard of such a thing! No, I will not pose as model for you. Why do you allow this silly business to come into the brain of her? Huh? Ach, poor little Miss Johnsy!"

"She's very ill and weak," said Sue. "The fever has filled her mind with strange thoughts. Very well, Mr. Behrman. If you don't want to pose, you needn't. But I think you're a horrible old————"

"You are just like a woman!" yelled Behrman. "Who says I not pose. Go on. I come with you. What a place is this city! One so good as Miss Johnsy should not lie sick. Some day I paint a masterpiece. Then we shall all go away. Yes?"

Johnsy was sleeping when they went upstairs. Sue pulled the shade down. She led Behrman into the other room. There they stared out the window at the ivy vine. They looked at each other for a moment. Neither spoke. A cold rain was now falling, mixed with snow. Behrman, in his old blue shirt, sat down to pose.

Sue slept badly that night. In the morning, she awoke from only an hour's sleep. She found Johnsy with dull, wide-open eyes. They were staring at the drawn green shade.

"Pull the shade up," Johnsy ordered. It was almost a whisper. "I want to see."

Tiredly, Sue obeyed.

But, there! A fierce wind had blown all night. The rain had beat down. Yet one ivy leaf stood out against the brick wall. Just one. It was still dark green near its stem. It's saw-tooth edge was tinted with yellow. It hung bravely about twenty feet from the ground.

"It's the last one," said Johnsy. "I thought it would fall during the night. I heard the wind. It will surely fall today, and I will die at the same time."

"No, no!" said Sue. She leaned her worried face down to the pillow. "Think of me, if you won't think of yourself. What would I do?"

But Johnsy did not answer. She seemed to be making ready to go on a mysterious, far journey. One by one, the ties that bound her to friendship and to earth were breaking.

The day wore away. At last came the twilight. They could still see the lone ivy leaf clinging to its stem. And then, with the coming of night, they could see it against the wall no longer. The north wind was again set free. The rain still beat against the windows.

The night passed slowly. When it was light enough, Johnsy spoke aloud. She ordered that the shade be raised.

The ivy leaf was still there.

Johnsy lay for a long time looking at it. Sue finally left for the kitchen. And then Johnsy called to Sue, who stopped stirring the chicken soup at once.

"I've been a bad girl, Susie," Johnsy said. "Something

has made that last leaf stay there. Why? To show me how wicked I was. It's a sin to want to die. You can bring me a little soup now. And some milk. No! Bring me a hand mirror first. Then pack some pillows behind me. I want to sit up."

An hour later she said:

"Susie, some day I'm going to paint the Bay of Naples."

The doctor came in the afternoon. Again, Sue followed him into the hallway as he left.

"Even chances," said the doctor. He took Sue's thin, shaking hand in his. "With good nursing you'll win. And now I must see another case. Behrman, his name is. He lives downstairs. Some kind of an artist, I think. Pneumonia, too. He's an old, weak man, and the disease is too much for him. There's no hope. But he goes to the hospital today. At least he'll be more comfortable."

The next day the doctor returned. "She's out of danger," he said to Sue. "You've won. Good food and care now—that's all."

And that afternoon Sue came to the bed where Johnsy lay. "I have something to tell you, white mouse," she said. Johnsy looked up from her knitting.

"Mr. Behrman died of pneumonia today," Sue went on. "He was ill only two days. They found him on the morning of the first day. He was in his room, helpless with pain. His clothes were wet and cold. They couldn't imagine where he'd been on such a bad night. And then they found a lantern, still lighted. Near it was a ladder. They found some scattered brushes, and some green and yellow paint. . . . Look out the window, Johnsy. Look at the last ivy leaf on the wall. Didn't you wonder why it never moved when the wind blew? Yes, it's Behrman's masterpiece. He painted it there the night that the last leaf fell!"

Recall

1. "Mr. Pneumonia" is (a) the doctor (b) a disease (c) an unhappy bill collector
2. At first, the doctor thinks Johnsy's chances to live are (a) very poor (b) about fifty-fifty (c) quite good
3. Sue tells Johnsy that her chances to live are (a) very poor (b) about fifty-fifty (c) quite good
4. Behrman enters the young women's studio to (a) care for Johnsy (b) pose for Sue (c) pull the shade down
5. The next morning, Johnsy is truly surprised to see (a) rain on the window (b) Sue (c) one last leaf
6. We learn later that the leaf had been (a) wired on the vine (b) painted by Behrman (c) put in Sue's scrapbook

Infer

7. The doctor in the story clearly believes that (a) the mind influences the body (b) most medicines are without value (c) all sick persons should be put in a hospital
8. The author suggests that Sue and Johnsy (a) are very rich (b) haven't quite enough money (c) are really too poor to live happily
9. Behrman's manner of talking indicates that he (a) doesn't know English too well (b) is always drunk (c) hates all women
10. At the end of the story, Sue calls the leaf "Behrman's masterpiece." She says this because (a) all Behrman's friends can now leave New York (b) the leaf saved a life (c) she has a cruel sense of humor

Vocabulary Review

1. A beginning artist is least likely to have a (a) *canvas* (b) *masterpiece* (c) *studio*
2. "Mr. Higgins *stalked* into the *studio.*" In other words, Mr. Higgins (a) bought into the business (b) walked into the workshop (c) turned into the kitchen
3. The _____ was painted on a large _____. The two terms that best fill the blanks are (a) *masterpiece . . . canvas* (b) *model . . . studio* (c) *funeral director . . . model*
4. The two words that have nothing to do with art are (a) *canvas, model* (b) *masterpiece, studio* (c) *pneumonia, stalk*

Critical Thinking

1. Because of its popularity "The Last Leaf" has been reprinted many times. One textbook has a picture of the leaf painted on the window, not on the brick wall. Do you think this is correct? Where do *you* think the leaf was painted? Use your common sense and refer to the story itself.
2. Do you think Sue was at all involved in Mr. Behrman's plan? Why, or why not? Refer to information from the story itself.
3. Did you foresee the end of the story before the last paragraph? There are several clues to the ending. Look back for two of them.

41

4. Explain this statement: " 'The Last Leaf' is a story of sacrifice. An old man with no future sacrifices his life for the life of a young woman whose future may be bright." Do you think this is the real meaning of the story? Why, or why not?

5. If you were Johnsy, what would be your thoughts at the end? Would you feel guilty? Explain.

Only the Guilty Run

Vin Packer

The next time you go to the library, here's a name to remember: M. E. Kerr. Maybe you've read one of her books already. If so, you already know a secret. M. E. Kerr can write about young people as though she were still quite young herself. And if you haven't read M. E. Kerr, get started tomorrow. Look on the library shelves. Look in the card catalog. Ask your librarian.

Why all this talk about M. E. Kerr? Simply because she also writes under the name "Vin Packer." "Only the Guilty Run" should make you a Kerr/Packer fan forever.

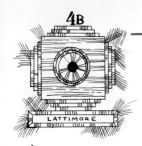

Vocabulary Preview

MOPE (MOPE) to act in a sad, slow-moving way
  • If I don't feel well, I'll just *mope* around the house on Saturday.

RUFFLED (RUF uld) patted or rubbed in a rough, playful way
  • Sam hated it when people *ruffled* his curly hair.

SARCASTICALLY (sar KAS tik lee) spoken in a manner intended to hurt
  • "That's terrific, Jim," the teacher said *sarcastically* as he returned the failing paper.

SAUCY (SAW-see) gay, lively
  • Her freckles and upturned nose gave her face a *saucy* look.

SENSITIVE (SEN si tiv) tender; easily hurt
  • Jim was *sensitive* about being so tall.

SONNET (SAHN it) a kind of 14-line poem
  • Vicky memorized a *sonnet* by Shakespeare.

WISTFUL (WIST ful) sad and wishful
  • Little Trina looked with *wistful* eyes at the toys she couldn't have.

I

T WAS A FEW HOURS AFTER DINNER, THAT cool evening at the beginning of September. Charlie got up from the big stuffed chair in the living room. He walked into the hall. He opened the closet and grabbed his red sweater. He said nothing to his parents. And they said nothing to him.

His mother had looked up from her work. Her smile was almost a question, and Charlie had winked in answer. His father had not taken his eyes from the ball game on TV. It was understood that they would not ask him where he was going. They would not demand to know what time he would return. This was his sixteenth summer. When the new school year started, Charlie would be a senior. If he wanted to, he could even smoke in front of his family. He had done so once. In July he had camped out for two weeks. With four of his best buddies, he had gone far up into the mountains. And other things had happened too. His allowance was increased to fifteen dollars a month. As long as he did not run short, he did not have to account for the money. After Labor Day, he would go to work from four until eight in Allen's Drugstore. He would open a savings account in the bank where his father worked.

Charlie stood in the hallway of the apartment building. He pushed the elevator button. Little Billy Crandell's mother was standing in front of 3C yelling. "C'mon now, Billy. It's after eight. Billy, I said hurry!" Billy was climbing up the stairs slowly. His coat dragged on the cement steps. His dark eyes were sad. He passed Charlie, and Charlie ruffled the boy's yellow hair. Charlie smiled to himself. He could remember when he was only that age.

Now he was downstairs in the lobby. He paused before the large square mirror. He was tall, and not skinny any more. His shoulders were broad. His legs and arms were all muscle, hard. The deep tan gave his face a strong, masculine look. It set off his gray eyes and made his teeth look very white when he grinned. The short haircut helped too. He looked older than he had in June. Even though it had only been three months, he *knew* he looked older—acted older too. He wasn't a kid any longer. He was grown up. He was on his own.

Then he thought of her . . . Of course, he had never really stopped thinking of her. Not all summer. He had pretended to himself that she was not important. He had told himself that she was just a stage he was going through, that it did not matter now. But in his heart he knew differently. It was crazy the way he had dreamed of her those days and nights. It had gone on through June, July, and August too. In his sleep he would see her entering the classroom again. He would see her smile. The dimples in her cheeks. The sparkling green eyes. The soft, long, pale-yellow hair touching her shoulders. He had seen her that way many times. But when he dreamed of it, he made it different. She called the roll the way she always did, but when she came to his name, she stopped and looked up. She searched the room for him. Then, when their eyes met, a wistful look came over her face. She said, "Oh, *there* you are." The tone in her voice was thrilled and tender. What she was really saying was, "Charlie, Charlie, I've missed you *so!*"

He would always wake up from that dream feeling thrilled himself. He would sing "I'll Be Seeing You" in the shower. He would shine his scratched-up brown shoes. Then he would take a long walk, humming to himself and watching the sky. It didn't matter that it was only a dream.

It didn't matter that Miss Lattimore had never said anything of the kind to him. It was wonderful, wasn't it? He was in love with her. She was his high-school English teacher. She was probably past twenty-seven, and he was just sixteen— but that didn't matter either. Those mornings after the dream were special. He believed only in his love, in Jill—that was her name. Miss Jill Lattimore.

Sometimes he was sad. He did not always sing or hum or smile. He did not always think it was wonderful to be alive. He read poetry, especially the plays and sonnets of Shakespeare. He imitated the way she had read them aloud in class.

> *How like a winter hath my absence been,*
> *From thee—*

That was the one he read most of the time. Then he would close the book. He would hold his head in his hands and say, "Jill!" and then, "Jill! If you only knew. . . ."

Charlie shook his head and stared at the mirror. How long had he been standing in the lobby, thinking of her? He didn't know. Suddenly he laughed and said to the mirror, "Shakespeare! *Me* a Shakespeare? Ha!" He shrugged his shoulders. "Yeah, *me.* Me—Charlie Wright. I like Shakespeare, that's all. And because of her!" He laughed again, but his stomach did a flip. When he walked out the door of the building, he was frowning.

It was getting dark. Charlie looked toward the end of the block. There were some kids sitting on the curb under a streetlight. He began to walk in the opposite direction. He went up the winding road of Overlook Terrace to Fort Washington Avenue. He had always liked living in Washington Heights. It was close to the river and the George Washington Bridge. Often he used to sit on the low bank near the water. He would watch the boats and barges go by. Last year he had found another reason for liking Washington Heights. Miss Lattimore lived on Cabrini Boulevard. Her building was a few blocks from where Charlie was walking right at that moment.

He had gone by the Excelsior Apartments dozens of times. Once he had gone inside and read her name on the mailbox. *Lattimore—4B.* Later he stood for a time in the road behind her building. He picked out her apartment from all the others. It was in the rear, facing the Hudson River. Sometimes in the early evening he would see the lights up there. He would wonder what she was doing. He would make a bet with himself. "If she comes to the window and looks out, she feels the same way I do." . . . But she never came to the window. Charlie had to go home sorrowfully. He would mope around in his room, angry at his mother's questions.

His mother would say, "Do you feel all right, dear?"

"Sure," Charlie answered. "Swell!" He would say it very sarcastically.

"Darling, if anything's the matter. . . ."

"Aw, for Pete's sake," he would exclaim. "For Pete's sake, Mom."

Then before he went to bed he would go to his mother. He would pat her under the chin with his finger and say, " 'Night, sweetheart. Pleasant dreams." Because he was always sorry when he was rude to her. When you came right down to it, he had a swell family. His mother and dad always played square with him. He used to think, "Why, I can tell them anything—*anything!*" But he couldn't tell them about this. This was different. He was in love—desperately in love—with an older woman. And he had been in love with her for one whole year.

Even the guys at school didn't know. He made sure of that. Some of the boys used to say, "Hey, that Lattimore is some chick, huh? All teachers should have *her* looks." Charlie would smile and tell them they were crazy. He cut up in her class. He shot paper airplanes across the room and whistled "La Cucaracha" when she read poetry. One day she kept him after class.

"Charlie," she said, "why can't we get along?"

He wanted to cry right then and there.

He said, "What difference does it make?"

"It makes a great deal of difference to me," she answered quietly. "You know, Charlie, I really do read the papers you write. I read them carefully. I think we both know you don't act the way you feel inside. You're quite a sensitive young man, Charlie. You write beautifully about beautiful things."

He thought, if she doesn't stop saying my name like that I *will* cry. If she doesn't stop saying things like that I *will* cry—I just won't be able to help myself.

He said roughly, "I'll be late for my next class."

"Please think it over," Miss Jill Lattimore said.

The truth was, she understood him. She understood him, and no one else really did. "*You're quite a sensitive young man, Charlie. You write beautifully about beautiful things.*" And what else had she said? That he didn't act the way he felt inside. He should have said, "Yes, Miss Lattimore. 'All the world's a stage, and all the men and women merely players.' " He should have said something adult. Adult and intelligent—like something Shakespeare had written. She was a bug on Shakespeare, and Charlie was too now. He had thumbed through the pocket-book Shakespeare he owned.

49

He had kept it under his pillow until the pages were worn and marked. . . .

This year it will be different, Charlie thought now. He walked along Fort Washington Avenue, past the drugstore. Inside, the gang was crowded in booths. They were listening to the jukebox and drinking Cokes. He didn't want to go into the drugstore. Who wanted to hear all that kid talk? He wanted to be by himself and think about the year ahead. How different it was going to be! He was grown up now and he would act grown up. Jill would notice it right away. He wasn't going to clown around any more. The very first morning of class he would go to her. He would say, "You know, Miss Lattimore, I was something of a buffoon last year." *Buffoon* was a good word. An adult word. It meant the kind of person who does anything for a laugh. And then he would quote from Shakespeare. "My salad days, when I was green in judgment." That would do it. Short and to the point. With a few words by Shakespeare and a sincere smile. He had been practicing sincere smiles all summer.

Charlie thought about how lucky he was. Miss Lattimore taught both junior and senior English. Two years with her—that *was* lucky! He might never have seen her again. Or heard her voice. Or watched the proud way she walked with her head held high, the tilt to her nose giving her face a saucy look. He was a lot taller than she was. And really, when he thought about it, she seemed younger than he. It was a fact that she didn't *look* twenty-seven. She didn't look that old at all.

There was a moon up over the Hudson now. Dots of light marked the New Jersey side of the river. Charlie walked on slowly. He made his hands into fists. He had not seen her for three months. He remembered what she had said about her summer. She would spend it in Colorado with her folks. School began in three days and she should be back. He turned and walked down Cabrini Boulevard. *"How like a winter hath my absence been, From thee."*

He stopped next to the building where she lived. And when he looked up, he saw the lights there. She was back! There was a drum in his stomach. He could feel his knees weaken. He did a strange thing. He kept walking toward the rear of the building until he could touch the brick with his hand. He touched it very gently. . . . Then he saw the fire escape. He said in a whisper to himself, "Don't be crazy, Charlie. Hey, don't be crazy!"

It was easy because he wore sneakers on his feet. He went up the iron steps like a cat. He was afraid too. He had never done anything like this in his life. Somehow, the moment was not quite real. The moon was bright and big, and when he looked down he felt dizzy. He kept thinking, "Go back"—but he wanted to see her.

He kept going. Soon he came to the fourth level. At the windows of 4B he went down on one knee. He lifted his head slowly to stare into the room. She was not there. He saw the bookcases. A wide gray rug. Modern lamps and low tables, and a black vase of flowers. *Her* room. Her living room. He just kept looking at it, trying to imagine her there.

Then everything happened.

He remembered the sudden flash of light. The sound of a loud voice ordering him to halt. The mad rush up the fire escape to the fifth floor and the sixth. His hands shook. His legs kept pulling him down. He thought he would fall. He wished he could jump. After he had gone three flights up, he stopped and held on to the wall of the building.

Two shots rang out in the night. Charlie screamed, terrified. He stood against the brick wall, sobbing, saying "No!" aloud. A dark figure came quietly toward him, grabbed the back of his sweater, jerked him forward. He felt the rough cloth of a police officer's coat. Again, he looked down. The sight made him dizzy. He felt himself go limp and the voice grew faint. . . .

"He's a good boy, a *good* boy." It was his mother's voice. Charlie sat slumped in a wooden chair at the Police Station. He heard his mother defend him, his father question him. A fat Police Captain in shirtsleeves stood next to Charlie, his face kindly, his eyes dark and serious.

"Try to explain, Son," Charlie's father said. "What made you go up there? Try to explain before Miss Lattimore comes."

Charlie couldn't answer. He kept thinking that he was very nearly killed.

"Were there any other boys with you?" the Captain asked. "We got a report saying there was only one."

"He's an Eagle Scout," his mother said. She spoke to everyone, and to no one. Her eyes were tired and red.

"Don't you like Miss Lattimore?" His father's tone was patient, soft. "Chuck, did you really go up there to look in *her* window?"

The officer broke in. "That's where he was, all right. Kneeling right outside her window."

Charlie knew he would cry out again any moment. There was a knot in his throat.

"I fired over his head," the officer said. "But it was dangerous just the same. He could have got it if he'd kept on running."

"What about it, Chuck?" his father said. "Try to tell us, Son."

He had almost been shot down, Charlie thought. Like

a criminal! He was dreaming, he would wake up. . . .

When he heard Miss Lattimore's voice, his hands went cold. His lips quivered. He could not have spoken if he had wanted to. He sat shaking.

"He's a good boy," his mother repeated. And Charlie thought, "Aw Mom, dear Mom." He kept his head lowered. That way, they couldn't see that his eyes were filled.

"I know he is," he heard Miss Lattimore say.

"We're sorry about this," his father apologized.

Charlie could not look up at her. He could not stop his shoulders from heaving with the great sobs inside him. He was just a kid after all, he told himself. Just a big sissy.

"I should have asked the super," Miss Lattimore began. "Or one of the boys that works in the building. But I never thought Charlie would be hurt doing me that favor."

"You mean?" Charlie's mother cried out.

"My TV wires. The nails were loose. It's attached to the window on the outside. But I didn't think he'd hurt himself. I certainly never thought that *this* would happen. Was he really reported for being a peeping Tom?"

Then Charlie looked up. He stared at her. She looked so little, standing there in her sky-blue dress. A sweater, the same color as her hair, lay over her shoulders.

"He was doing you a favor?" his mother asked. Her voice was full of hope.

"That's right," Miss Lattimore answered, "I met him on the street and asked him if he would. I just returned yesterday. There's so much work, getting settled in again and—"

She's beautiful, he thought. She's like an angel.

"Well," the Captain boomed out. "That ends that!"

"Chuck, you should have said so." His father was smiling broadly. His arm was around Charlie's shoulder. "Son, you should have spoken up, told us about it."

Miss Lattimore was holding her eyes steady with Charlie's. "He was probably afraid," she said carefully. "He could have been killed."

She had done this thing for him. She had understood. She had known. And she had done this thing for him. . .

"Never run," the officer said at the door. "Only guilty people run, my boy."

"Your postcards got through to me, Charlie," Miss Lattimore said. "You seem to have had a nice summer." They were leaving the Police Station now—Miss Lattimore, Charlie, his mother and father.

His mother said, "He went camping with some other boys. They were alone in the woods. He's sixteen now, you know."

He didn't mind his mother saying that. For some reason he didn't mind.

His father said, "I have my car, Miss Lattimore. May I drop you off?"

In the car everyone began to laugh. It wasn't really funny, his mother said. After all, he could have been killed. Charlie laughed too. Here he was, sitting in the back seat looking at Jill's light blond hair. At last she waved goodbye to them in front of her building. Charlie watched her walk to the door. He watched her disappear from sight. Then he sat forward. He rested his chin on the back of the seat where his parents sat, and he kept thinking about her. . . .

It was near midnight. He had waited for the house to be still. Finally he heard the door to his parents' room close. Quickly and quietly he moved down the hall. He went down the steps to the lobby, and out into the street. The late night air was colder now. He wished he had brought his coat, instead of just wearing his suit. His only suit—dark blue and almost new.

The streets were empty. The stores along Fort Washington Avenue were dark. Soon he came to Cabrini Boulevard. This time he did not turn down the back road. He walked right up to the entrance of her building. A man with a skinny dog held the door open for Charlie. Once inside, he took the elevator to the fourth floor.

When she answered the door, he said, "Hello, Jill."

She stood there in a fuzzy white robe. Her long hair was pulled behind her ears and held with a red ribbon. Her eyes were wide, her lips half parted. She looked at him with disbelief.

"Aren't you going to ask me in?" he said.

She blocked the entrance. "Charlie Wright, go home. Now!"

"Jill," he said. "Listen, Jill—"

"Charlie, what on earth? Don't you realize that I was trying to be a good sport tonight? I was trying to help you, Charlie. Don't you *realize* that?"

"Why?" he said. "Why were you helping me?" He made his lips grin playfully, but he was less sure now.

"You poor kid. Please, Charlie, go home! Don't you see? I was trying to help you. I was trying because I knew you had a crush on me. All those postcards. And the silly way you acted in my class last year. And the papers you wrote. Charlie, please! Don't make me do anything mean."

He didn't know what to do. He felt foolish standing before her. Here he was in his blue suit with his new shirt and striped tie. He said "Crush?" and his voice did not sound like his own.

"Charlie, leave right now. I mean it." Her eyes were round. As he looked into them, he suddenly knew that something was terribly wrong. She was afraid of him. She was really afraid of his being there.

He said, "Look, I won't hurt you. I only want to— I want, I —" He began to stutter. He felt confused. He wanted everything to be all right. He wanted to make whatever he was doing all right. She wasn't in love with him. He wanted to make that all right too, and it was. It really was. Because he didn't love her either, any more. In those slow seconds he woke up to the horrible truth. But it was all right. All he wanted to do now was to go home. He wanted to get some sleep. Then he would get up and find the gang tomorrow. Play ball. Go to the drugstore. Things like that. He wasn't Charlie Wright standing before the door of his English teacher's apartment. That was crazy.

"Go on, now!" She raised her voice. The sound startled him. But he knew the truth. He didn't want anything more to happen to make things worse. He reached out, without really knowing what he was doing. But he had to stop the words she was saying to him. He had to tell her that he was sorry, that he was a fool, and was going.

He put his hand across her mouth. Right away, she screamed. She screamed the way he had when the shots had rung out on the fire escape.

He said, "Listen—I—" But it was too late. The man from the next apartment was in the hall. He was running toward Charlie. Charlie stood still. Miss Lattimore was crying, and the man had Charlie by the shoulder.

"Miss Lattimore," he tried to say again. But she was sobbing her words wildly now. She was telling the man that Charlie was a foolish kid. That he had a crush on her. That she couldn't control him. That this time he had gone too far. . . . Charlie knew that in minutes the police would be on their way. Before long, the phone would ring out in the darkness of his parents' room. Now he was on his own—really on his own.

Recall

1. At the beginning of the story, we are told that Charlie enjoys (a) his many girlfriends (b) the feeling of being grown up (c) fooling his parents
2. Charlie is best described as a (a) career-minded student (b) stuck-up kid (c) dreamer
3. Charlie has nearly persuaded himself that (a) Miss Lattimore loves him (b) Shakespeare was a poor poet (c) he should ask to be put in another English class
4. When Charlie sees the light in Miss Lattimore's window, he (a) thinks of Romeo and Juliet (b) calls her on the phone (c) climbs the fire escape
5. The big surprise at the Police Station is that (a) Charlie's parents are on his side (b) Charlie confesses (c) Miss Lattimore lies to protect Charlie
6. As they leave the Police Station, words very much like the story's title are spoken by (a) Miss Lattimore (b) the police officer (c) Charlie
7. Charlie returns to Miss Lattimore's apartment as soon as (a) he's sure she's reached home (b) his parents close their door (c) she gives the signal
8. Charlie is surprised to find that Miss Lattimore's feeling for him is (a) not love but fear (b) hatred (c) too beautiful for words

9. Charlie grabs Miss Lattimore to (a) kiss her (b) make her stop talking a minute (c) frighten her

10. At the end of the story, it's clear that Charlie will soon be (a) home (b) in Miss Lattimore's apartment (c) back at the Police Station.

Infer

11. Although the location of the story is never mentioned, several clues indicate that it is (a) New York City (b) Detroit (c) Washington, D.C.

12. Charlie's cutting up in Miss Lattimore's class was probably caused by his (a) desire to make her life miserable (b) need for any kind of attention from her (c) dislike of English class

13. "How like a winter hath my absence been, From thee." In this quotation, the word *winter* suggests (a) the school year (b) Christmas and New Year's holidays (c) sadness

14. When Charlie looks up and sees the lights in Miss Lattimore's apartment, we are told that "there was a drum in his stomach." The word *drum* suggests a (a) barrel (b) victory parade (c) tight, pounding feeling

15. At the Police Station, the person who probably never realizes that Miss Lattimore lied is (a) the police officer (b) Charlie's mother (c) Charlie himself

16. Charlie makes a mistake when he believes that (a) Miss Lattimore's kindness means that she loves him (b) his parents really trust him (c) he looks older than he did in June

17. For what happens to Charlie at the end of the story, we can put most blame on (a) Miss Lattimore (b) Charlie himself (c) the parents

18. Charlie's mother can best be described as (a) careless and selfish (b) loving and concerned (c) lighthearted and thoughtless
19. Twice in the story, Charlie seems unable to (a) control his actions (b) trust other people (c) make up his mind about finishing school
20. Most readers of the story probably (a) think the teacher was horribly unfair (b) see Charlie as an evil person (c) feel sorry for Charlie

Vocabulary Review

Write on your paper the term in *italics* that belongs in each blank. Use each term only once.

mope	*ruffled*	*sensitive*	*wistful*
saucy	*sarcastically*	*sonnet*	

1. "You eat like a bird, Tony," Mom said _____ as I took a third piece of pie.
2. Don't _____ about your problems; try to *do* something about them.
3. Hal's face was excited and his hair was all _____ up.
4. The comedian winked at the audience and gave them a big, happy, _____ smile.
5. A short, tender poem might be called a _____ _____.
6. Dad gave the neighbors's new car a _____ look.

59

Critical Thinking

1. Like most people, Charlie Wright isn't *all* good or *all* bad. What are at least two of his good points? What are at least two weaknesses?

2. Do you think Miss Lattimore did the right thing in the police station? Explain your answer. What else might she have done later to prevent what finally happened? Can she fairly be criticized for *not* doing this?

3. The end of the story (from the time Miss Lattimore came to the door) is very important. Read it again. Do you think Charlie really deserved what finally happened?

4. What do you think will happen now? What will Miss Lattimore have to admit to the police? If you were the police captain, how much of the blame for what happened would you put on Miss Lattimore? None? Ten percent? Fifty percent?

5. The end of the story has Charlie thinking that he's "really on his own." Is this completely true? Who might help him?

6. What does the title of the story mean? How might you make it a lesson for your own life?

7. The story has several meanings other than the one indicated by the title. Try to put what you think is the most important meaning in your own words.

SPOOKS
AND
SPIRITS

Ghosts were created when
the first man woke in the
night.

J. M. Barrie

The Mansion of the Dead

Jean Anderson

With this story, we start on the second of the book's three sections. It's called "Spooks and Spirits." Get ready for a few ghosts. That is, get ready if you can. You'll know more about ghosts when you've read the stories.

Most ghost stories, of course, are made up. But here's one that's absolutely true. Read now about the strange spirits that once haunted "The Mansion of the Dead."

Vocabulary Preview

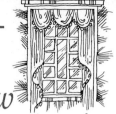

ACRE (AY kur) a measure of land
- The playing area of a football field covers about one *acre* of land.

CUPOLA (KUE puh luh) a small dome or tower on top of a roof
- The *cupola* on the barn lets air in and out.

MANSION (MAN shun) a large, expensive house
- The Ballard's *mansion* recently sold for $750,000.

MEDIUM (MEE dee um) a person who claims to be in touch with spirits of the dead
- Through a *medium,* Mr. Paul thought he spoke to his dead wife.

MORBID (MORE bid) very sad and depressed; unhealthy
- Living alone had made Mr. Paul *morbid* and ill.

SEANCE (SAY ans) a planned meeting with spirits of the dead
- During the *seance,* a table rose in the darkened room and three spirits appeared.

UNINHABITED (un in HAB uh tid) not inhabited, not lived in
- Except for ghosts, the old, lonely house was *uninhabited.*

CALIFORNIA'S SANTA CLARA VALLEY IS just south of San Francisco. There stands a five-million-dollar mansion. It is empty. The rooms contain little furniture. It is uninhabited—except by spirits of the dead. It is Winchester House, a huge, winding mansion built entirely for ghosts. Its strange story begins about 100 years ago in New Haven, Connecticut.

During the late 1800s, the name of Winchester had the same meaning as "rifle." And it is with the Winchester family that this story deals. With Sarah Winchester, to be exact. She was married to the wealthy son of the "Rifle King." No one knows whether Sarah Winchester was born with "second sight." She may have had a natural ability to get in touch with those beyond the grave. Or she may have developed that ability after tragedy struck.

Tragedy did strike Sarah Winchester—a swift, double blow. Within a few short months she lost not only her husband but also her only child. And, it seemed to friends, her mind as well. Sarah withdrew behind closed windows and doors. As the weeks passed, she grew more and more morbid. The doctors she saw were unable to cure or comfort her. She retreated into the world of spirits. She invited mediums to her home. Through seances, she hoped, she could again join her dead husband, William, and her daughter. Time and again mediums came. And went, without having reached William. Sarah then heard about an unusual medium in Boston. His name was Adam Coons. He had had special success in reaching the dead. Sarah went to Coons, without giving him her real name. He told her that her husband was standing beside her.

"Tell him that I miss him terribly," she said.

"He wants you to know that he is with you," Coons replied. "And he will always be with you." Then he gave Sarah a message from the spirit world. That message would change her life completely.

"This is a warning," the medium said. His voice seemed to float on the air. "There are many ghosts of those who have been killed by Winchester rifles. They will haunt you forever unless you do the right thing by them. . . ."

She was to sell her New Haven home. Then she was to move west. There she would buy a new home, which her dead husband would point out. She was to rebuild the house, "making room in it for all these spirits." Sarah must continue to build, Coons added. If she did, she would live —with William nearby.

The seance excited Sarah. She returned to New Haven at once. She sold her house and journeyed cross-country to California. Here she wandered for weeks. She searched the towns and the countryside. The mountains and valleys. The forests and deserts. Where was the house that William wanted? Money was no problem. Sarah had a fortune worth some $20,000,000. In addition, money came from the rifle company at about $1,000 a day.

Finally, in the peaceful Santa Clara Valley, Sarah found the house. It was a plain eight-room building on 44 acres of farmland. "This is it," a ghostly voice said. And she knew that William had spoken.

Sarah bought the farm. Then she set about her strange job of changing the house. She had to make space for the hundreds of ghosts of those killed by Winchester rifles. She hired 18 servants and an army of builders. Carpenters. Plumbers. Plasterers. Stone workers. Painters. Glass cutters. For 36 years these workers followed Sarah's strange commands. They built up and they tore down. They changed rooms and built additions. In the end the house stretched out over six acres of ground. One worker spent 30 years building cupolas. Another spent 33 years laying fancy floors and ripping them up again.

The sound of hammers and saws never stopped. Rooms were tacked onto rooms. Additions went out at odd angles. Stairways aimed into thin air. There were, finally, 2,000 doors. (Many opened onto blank walls.) There were 160 rooms. There were 47 fireplaces and 40 stairways. There were dozens of hallways that led nowhere and secret passageways.

As the work went on, Sarah became oddly interested in the number 13. Each ceiling had to have 13 sections. Each room had to have 13 windows. Each stairway had to have 13 steps. (One stairway, however, is different. It is divided, for some reason, into seven flights and 44 steps. And it climbs only 10 feet from one floor to the next!)

Sarah spent 36 years at Winchester House. She received three famous visitors. President Theodore Roosevelt had been a close friend of her husband's. Mary Baker Eddy had started the Christian Science Church. Harry Houdini, the magician, was the third. Her most honored guests, however, were the ghosts. It was for them she was building Winchester House. For them she built a windowless seance room. This was the small and secret Blue Room.

Each midnight, dressed in long robes, Sarah retreated to the Blue Room. There she received her friends from the spirit world. They were called by the ringing of a tower bell. Sarah also gave dinner parties for a dozen phantom guests. (There were always 12, so that with Sarah there were 13 at table.) The food was amazing. Master cooks brought over from Europe prepared the long feasts. The dinners continued year after year. Always, they were attended by guests only Sarah could see.

Sarah's life ended in September 1922. At the age of 85, she passed into the world of spirits she both loved and feared. She left Winchester House to a niece. She also left strict instructions that her guests of years past continue to be welcome. Later, the niece sold the house. But the new owners had to promise to obey the instructions.

Her wishes are still obeyed. Winchester House is kept in good repair. By day it is open to tourists. Guides take small groups through a section of the house. Most of the rooms, however, are closed off.

They belong to Sarah and to the night.

Recall

1. Sarah Winchester's fortune was the result of her (a) belief in the spirit world (b) marrying into a wealthy family (c) success as president of a company that made rifles

2. The story makes it clear that Sarah's interest in the spirit world was brought about by the efforts of (a) her husband William (b) her daughter (c) Sarah herself

3. The mansion was built as a home for (a) all ghosts (b) ghosts of people who had been killed by Winchester rifles (c) ghosts of famous people

4. The Blue Room was (a) the largest room in the mansion (b) the room in which President Roosevelt slept (c) the place where Sarah met with the spirits

5. When Sarah died, the mansion (a) continued to be run according to her instructions (b) was turned into a hotel (c) was left empty because of the ghosts

Infer

6. Certain things in the story indicate that Sarah Winchester was (a) totally insane (b) totally sane (c) willing to believe what made her feel better
7. Most people today would probably believe that Adam Coons, the medium, was a (a) genius (b) liar (c) ghost
8. It is clear from the story that (a) its author, Jean Anderson, believes in ghosts (b) many people saw ghosts in the mansion (c) Sarah believed in ghosts
9. If you visited Winchester House next summer, you would probably (a) see all the rooms (b) see only the Blue Room (c) see only some of the rooms
10. It makes most sense to wish that (a) Sarah had had some better way of spending her money (b) the workers had all come from North America (c) Adam Coons had married Sarah

Vocabulary Review

1. An *uninhabited mansion* is the same thing as a (a) haunted castle (b) large, empty house (c) happy-go-lucky way of life
2. If you believed in communication with the dead, you might ask a (a) *seance* to hold a *medium* (b) *medium* to hold a *cupola* (c) *medium* to hold a *seance*
3. Many people have trouble remembering the size of an *acre* of land. You won't have trouble if you keep in mind a (a) city block (b) large parking lot (c) football field
4. A *morbid* person would probably not (a) laugh a lot (b) eat meat (c) worry about things
5. A *cupola* would not be a good place for a (a) square dance (b) lightning rod (c) weather vane

Critical Thinking

1. Sarah Winchester's early life was unfortunate, but she was partly to blame for what happened to her later. What was the challenge that Sarah was unable to meet?

2. Sarah's troubles started a little over 100 years ago. Had she been born 100 years later, her life would probably have been quite different. Why? (Hint: Think about such things as (a) income and other taxes (b) opportunities for women (c) popularity of mediums.)

3. One of Sarah's guests was Harry Houdini, the famous magician. Throughout his life, Houdini was interested in the spirit world. But he was hardly a believer. He thought that all mediums were fakes. Whenever he could, he attended their seances. He loved discovering the tricks they used to make ghostly voices, shapes, and breezes. He offered a small fortune to any medium whose tricks he could not find and reveal. He made an agreement with a friend that whoever died first would try to contact the other. Do you think Houdini lost any money on his offer? Do you think the dead ever communicate with the living? Several books about Houdini will tell you his findings.

4. The introduction to the story stated that it was "absolutely true." This statement, of course, is not quite right. What kinds of things in the story are true? What kinds of things are probably not true?

Here It Is!

Donna Kaczmarsyk

*A traditional story is one that belongs to everyone
—and to no one. Traditional tales have been told
thousands of times by thousands of tellers. Like folk
tales, they belong to the people. Yet no one knows
how they started. No single person can be named as
author.*

*"Here It Is!" is such a tale. It deals with a
one-legged ghost and a worried young widow. It
starts with the shivers, but they lead to a laugh.
Here it is.*

71

Vocabulary Preview

EMBERS (EM burz) the red-hot coals of a dying fire
- The forest fire started from some *embers* left by campers.

PERISH (PER ish) to die
- Four firemen *perished* in the blaze.

PETRIFIED (PET ruh fide) turned to stone; made stiff by fear
- Miguel was *petrified* when he saw the ghost.

PLATINUM (PLAT uh num) a valuable silver-white metal
- The old-fashioned watch had a *platinum* case.

RIGID (RI jid) stiff; not moving
- The roar of the fire made me *rigid* with fear.

TRANSPARENT (trans-PAR-unt) capable of being seen through; clear
- Most window glass is *transparent* so people can see through it.

WIRY (WIR-ee) lean and strong
- The greyhound may seem thin, but the dog's body has much *wiry* strength.

THEY WERE SITTING AROUND THE CAMP-
fire, telling ghost stories. The hour was late. The fire had
died down. Seven red faces shone from the glow of the
embers. Beyond, the night was as black as a roomful of black
cats.

Maria finished a story about an armless spook. The
ghost had been defeated with a mirror. That was the way to
get rid of a ghost, she explained. "The next time you see a
ghost, you just hold a mirror up to it. Ghosts are scared of
ghosts. More scared than we are."

No one spoke. No one wanted to break the spell. Tomorrow, it was back to the city. And the next week, back
to another year of school.

Janet broke the silence: "Did you ever hear the story
about the wooden leg?"

No one had.

"Well," Janet began. She pulled her jacket tighter
around her shoulders. It was growing chilly. "Seems many
years ago there was this sea captain. He had a wooden leg."

"What happened to his real one?" Jack asked.

"It had been bit off," Janet said. "By a shark. Just below
the knee.

"Anyhow, this sea captain was very proud of his
wooden leg. It was specially made for him out of the hardest
wood. Everywhere he went, he carried some sandpaper with
him. Sandpaper and a little varnish. Just in case the leg got
nicked or something. The leg had a gold band on the top of
it. And a platinum tip at the bottom.

"And—oh, yes!—this captain had a beautiful young
bride. That's the way it always is in these stories. The sea

captains always have pretty young wives at home. In those days, the wives were supposed to be a little bit afraid of their husbands. But when the husbands went to sea, the poor little things always just moped around.

"Well, one day this young bride got some bad news. Really bad news. Her husband had drowned at sea. It was just the second day out. A bad storm had come up. Half the crew had perished in the waves.

"So there was a funeral and everything. Then the wife just moped and moped. No one could cheer her up. She used to go down to the sea and just sit there alone. Looking. Longing. Waiting. It was like, well————Like as if her looking could bring the captain back.

"Well, one day she was walking on the beach. And what do you think she found?"

"The wooden leg," Don said.

"The wooden leg!" Janet repeated. "It was almost a year. But the leg was as good as new. She carried it home. She couldn't take her hands off it. She ate supper with the thing in her lap. Then she carried it around in her arms, like a baby. When she went to bed, she put it under her pillow.

"But she didn't go to sleep right away. There was a storm that night. She lay there listening. The wind moaned in the chimney. The old house creaked. Mo-o-o-oan. Mo-o-o-oan. Cre-e-e-ek. Cre-e-e-ek. Under the pillow, her wiry fingers were clutching that leg.

"It was that way for hours. She'd fall half asleep. Then the wind would wake her up. And all the time, she kept her grip on the leg. It was very late when she thought she heard a click. Yes, she *did* hear it! It wasn't the house creaking. She knew that click. It was the door opening, downstairs.

"She tried to get up. But she couldn't. The door had a

good latch. The wind hadn't opened it. She knew that. Someone was in the house. But who?

"Then it came, the noise from downstairs. It was soft, and very slow:

"STEP . . . TAP . . . STEP . . . TAP . . . STEP . . . TAP . . . STEP . . . TAP.

"It was the ghost! Come back to get his leg."

"To *get* his leg?" said Maria. "The ghost had to have the wooden leg didn't it? I thought she *heard* the leg tapping."

"Of course she did," said Janet. "But that was the *ghostly* leg. The one she had was the *real* one.

"Then she heard it again, very slowly, softly:

"STEP . . . TAP . . . STEP . . . TAP . . . STEP . . . TAP . . .

"Now it was on the stairs!" Janet's voice became a slow whisper:

"STEP . . . TAP . . . STEP . . . TAP. The ghost stopped, resting. STEP . . . TAP.

"The poor girl was petrified. Rigid. Her hands were wet on the leg. She couldn't move. She couldn't breathe. The big house was creaking. The wind was moaning. Then she heard another moan. It was a ghostly voice, from far away, yet very near:

" 'GIVE . . . ME . . . BACK . . . MY . . . LEG!'

" 'GIVE . . . ME . . . BACK . . . MY . . . LEG!'

"Now it was walking down the hall:

"STEP . . . TAP . . . STEP . . . TAP.

" 'GIVE . . . ME . . . BACK . . . MY . . . LEG!'

"Her face was wet, her eyes big circles of fear. She felt a rush of air on her forehead. The door of her room creaked open. Cre-e-e-ek.

"At first she couldn't see the thing. Then, *there it was!* Ghostly white. Transparent. Standing in the doorway.

" 'GIVE ... ME ... BACK ... MY ... LEG!'

"The voice was hollow, haunting. It was just five steps to the bed:

"STEP ... TAP ... STEP ... TAP ... STEP.

"Now it was beside her, bending over, and. . . .

"HERE IT IS!"

The leg flew through the air. Everyone jumped. It landed in Don's lap. Don screamed and stood up.

In a minute everyone was laughing, even Don. At his feet lay the small stick of firewood that Janet had hidden under her jacket.

This story—or one very much like it—has been told thousands of times around thousands of fires. Try it sometime. Pause just before you say "HERE IT IS." Scream the words in a loud, frightened voice. You don't really need a campfire and a stick of wood. A dim room and a rolled up newspaper will do.

Recall

1. Early in the story, we are told that a ghost can be defeated with a (a) wooden leg (b) pail of water (c) mirror
2. The dead captain's wooden leg is found by (a) his son (b) his widow (c) some fishermen
3. The widow's feeling about the leg is one of (a) horror (b) attachment (c) joy in having the gold and platinum to sell
4. The purpose of the ghost's visit is to (a) cheer up the widow (b) kill the widow (c) get the leg
5. The "leg" that flies through the air at the end of the story is actually a (a) stone (b) piece of firewood (c) spoon

Infer

6. The story of Janet and her friends probably takes place in the (a) fall (b) winter (c) spring
7. Janet tells about the captain and his young bride (a) very seriously (b) with a lot of humor (c) in a bored way
8. The widow first knows that the ghost is her husband because of (a) his voice (b) the way he opens the door (c) the sound of his walk
9. Near the end of the story is the sentence "Everyone jumped." In truth, however, probably everyone jumped except (a) Janet (b) the widow (c) Don
10. The ending of the story proves that Janet (a) believes in ghosts (b) dislikes the other campers (c) tells a story well

Vocabulary Review

Below are *italicized* words from the story followed by sentences with blanks. On your paper, write the numeral of each sentence and the words that best fill the blanks. Use each word only once.

embers	*perish*	*platinum*	*wiry*
transparent	*petrified*	*rigid*	

1. Surely, you would rather hold _____ than _____ in your hand.
2. Two words with nearly the same meaning are _____ and _____.
3. All plants and all animals must someday _____.

4. Butchers wrap meats in _____ plastic so shoppers can see what they are buying.

5. The high jumper had long arms and thin, _____ legs.

Critical Thinking

1. The success of "Here It Is!" depends on the telling. Could you tell the story well? Reread the end of the story (from the click of the door opening) as though you were telling it. What parts should you read very slowly? Very fast? Softly? Loudly? Explain why in each case.

2. "Here It Is!" is actually two stories: 1) The story of Janet and her friends; 2) the story of the widow and the ghost. We might call these the 1) outer and 2) inner stories. Explain why the inner story was not used by itself in this book. Why was it better to have someone like Janet tell it?

3. Because of the surprise at the end, the inner story is never finished. It ends with an incomplete sentence:" 'Now it was beside her, bending over and. . . .' " Finish this sentence and write a good ending yourself.

4. Many other traditional ghost stories are very much like "Here It Is!" Tell and discuss some of these other tales you have heard. Compare them with "Here It Is!"

The Girl
in the Lavender Dress

Maureen Scott

The story that follows is of a special kind. It's a tall tale dressed up as "truth." Several such stories have been making the rounds in recent years.

There is, for instance, the story about the amazing new carburetor. A new car gets sixty miles to the gallon. The buyer tells the dealer. The buyer then gets a small fortune from the dealer. All he has to do is to keep quiet about the "secret new carburetor" he got by mistake. In actual fact, this story never happened. But people want to believe it. That's why it has spread by word of mouth from Maine to Vancouver.

But even stranger is the tale of "The Girl in the Lavender Dress." Let's read this "true" story now.

Vocabulary Preview

EDGY (EJ ee) on edge, nervous, jittery
- The sleepless night left me tired and *edgy.*

DECEASED (dee SEEST) no longer living; dead
- All of my grandparents are now *deceased.*

FUTILE (FYUT ul) useless, without result
- They spent all day in a *futile* search for the lost money.

INCREDIBLE (in CRED uh bul) hard, or impossible, to believe
- Most flying saucer stories are *incredible.*

LAVENDER (LAV un dur) a light purple color
- The *lavender* flowers filled the air with sweetness.

SPLOTCH (SPLOCH) a stain; an area with no regular shape
- The spilled soup left a large *splotch* on Toby's shirt.

M

Y GRANDMOTHER WAS, I ALWAYS BE-
lieved, a truthful woman. She paid her taxes. She went to
church. She considered the Lord's business as her own.
When her children told lies, they soon saw the light of truth.
They went to bed without any supper, the taste of soap still
sharp on their tongues.

That's why the story that follows bothers me so much.
It just *can't* be true. Of course, Grandma was ninety-two
when she told it to me. Her mind had started to fail. She
might have really believed it. Who knows? Maybe you will
too.

I'll try to tell the story just the way she told it to me.
She was in a nursing home then. It was late at night. The two
of us were alone in the TV room. Grandma's eyelids hung
low over her eyes. She worked her wrinkled jaw a few times
and began:

It all happened about '42 or '43 [Grandma said]. It
was during World War II. We didn't have much gas in
those days. No one did. So whenever Herbert took the
car somewhere, I tried to go along for the ride.

We lived in Vermont in those days. This time I'm
thinking of, Herbert had some business in Claremont.
That's in New Hampshire, just across the river. Well,
seems Herbert had saved up the gas to go by car. About
twenty-five miles. He said we could leave after work
Friday. That night we'd have us a good restaurant meal.

81

Maybe see a movie, too. Then we'd stay in a hotel and drive back the next day.

I don't remember the month, exactly. Sometime in the fall, 'cause it was cool. It was a misty night. I remember Herbert had to keep the wipers going. And it was after dusk when we first saw her. I know it was dark, 'cause I remember first seeing her in the lights ahead.

Neither Herbert nor I spoke. He slowed down, and the girl stopped walking. She just stood there on our side of the road. Not hitching, exactly. But she sure looked like she wanted a ride. It was a lonely road, and there weren't many cars.

First Herbert passed her, going real slow. Then he backed up to where she was. I rolled down my window. She was a pretty little thing, about eighteen or twenty. A round face, and big round eyes. Brown hair, cut straight. The mist kind of made her face shine. But the funny thing was what she was wearing. Only a thin lavender party dress. In that weather!

Well, I don't remember that anybody did any asking. I just opened the door. She climbed into the back seat. Herbert started up again. Finally I asked her where she was going.

"Claremont." That was all she said at first. She had a light, breathless voice. Like it took a whole lung full of air to say that one word.

"You're lucky," Herbert said. "We're going all the way."

The girl didn't reply. We rode on a little ways. I turned around once or twice, but the girl just smiled. Sort of sadly. Anyhow, I didn't want to stare at her. But who was she? Why was she walking on a lonely road

82

at night? I've never been the kind to pry into other people's business. So what I did then was, well, I'd taken off my sweater when the car got warm. I offered it to her, and she put it on.

The mist turned to light rain. Just before we got to the river, Herbert broke the silence. "Where are you going in Claremont, Miss?"

There was no reply.

"It's coming on to rain," Herbert said. "And we got time to deliver you."

"Oh," the girl breathed. "Could you *really?* That would be———— That would be *nice.* To my parents' house. Corner of Bond and Mason."

"Claremont must be a nice place to grow up," I said. But again, there was no sound from the back of the car. You couldn't even hear her breathing. I just settled back into my seat and enjoyed the trip. We crossed the bridge and headed into town. Then Herbert turned right onto Bond Street.

We rode along, looking at the street signs. Mason was way out. There was only one house on the corner, on the opposite side. Herbert made a U-turn and stopped the car.

There was no one in the rear seat!

I looked at Herbert. He looked at me, his eyes popping. I hunched up so I could see the back floor. Nothing. Just a little wetness where her feet had been.

"Where'd she get out?" Herbert asked.

"At a stoplight?" I wondered. But we both knew it couldn't be. It was a two-door car. We'd know it if a door opened. Both of us looked at the rear windows. They were closed, as they had been. Neither of us had felt a draft.

Yet there had to be some explanation. "Come," Herbert said. We hurried toward the house. It was a big, square box-like building. Lights were on in nearly every room. Splotches of brightness covered the wet lawn.

The door had a name on it: J. R. Bullard. It was opened by a long-faced man about fifty.

"Excuse me," Herbert said, "But there seems to be some mystery. You see, your daughter————"

"Daughter?" said the man. "Why, we don't have any daughter." A small woman, some years younger, now stood at his side.

"Well————" Herbert began.

"We *did* have a daughter," the woman said. "But Carol is deceased, you see. She was buried in Calhoun Cemetery four months ago."

Herbert gripped my arm. We both knew Calhoun Cemetery. It was on the Vermont side of the river. "Then who————?" Herbert wondered aloud. Suddenly he looked embarrassed. "Excuse us," he muttered. "It's all a—a mistake."

"Just a minute," I said. "Would you mind telling us what Carol looked like?"

The couple exchanged glances. If they were worried, it wasn't about Carol. It was about *us.* "A little on the short side," the woman said, almost to herself. "A round face. Big round eyes. Dark straight hair, cut in bangs."

Herbert's hand was a lobster claw on my elbow. We excused ourselves in a hurry. Back in the car, we sped away through the night. Then we drove around for hours, looking. Across the bridge. Down every little road. Back into Claremont. Near every stoplight. Along Bond Street.

But we both knew the search was futile. There was only one answer. What we'd had in our car, sitting on the back seat and even talking, was the ghost of Carol Bullard. And the amazing thing was that we had proof. A ghost, you see, cannot cross water. That was why, when we came to the river, the ghost had only one choice: to disappear!

Grandma stopped talking. I thought that was the end of her incredible story. But no. There was more:

And that isn't all [Grandma went on]. That night —the night that it happened—we were both pretty edgy. Didn't get much sleep, either. Not till the next morning did we think of my sweater. It had disappeared with the ghost.

That was a really good sweater. Almost new. You see, we didn't have much money. And it was wartime. Clothes were hard to come by. But once in a while I'd blow a week's pay on something really nice. Something that would last for years—like that sweater.

Now listen: it's like this. On the way home, we thought we'd swing around by Calhoun Cemetery. We wanted to find a certain gravestone. It would say "Carol Bullard" on it. So we did just that. It took a long time. But finally we found the new graves. And there, at last, was the stone. A small flat stone. Just "Carol Bullard" on it. No dates; nothing more. But next to the stone, neatly folded up, *was my sweater!*

True—or not? You decide.

Recall

1. The grandmother tells the story (a) at her home (b) in a nursing home (c) somewhere in Vermont
2. During the ride to Claremont, the grandmother was a little bothered by the girl's (a) ghostly smile (b) failure to speak much (c) back-seat driving
3. We learn from the story that ghosts (a) only appear in the fall (b) cannot talk (c) cannot cross water
4. The first real shock in the story comes when the girl (a) disappears (b) accepts the sweater (c) sees her parents
5. After learning about Carol from her parents, the grandmother and her husband (a) tell them about the ghost (b) ask for a photograph (c) leave hurriedly
6. The sweater is finally found (a) next to a tombstone (b) in the car (c) on Carol's back

Infer

7. We can assume that Carol Bullard was buried in a (a) long gown (b) lavender dress (c) sweater
8. "Herbert's hand was a lobster claw on my elbow." In other words, his hand (a) was red (b) was cold (c) had a very tight grip
9. After leaving the car, the "girl-ghost" in the story must have (a) gone to haunt her parents' home (b) gone to haunt the grandmother's home (c) returned to her grave
10. The grandmother seems to (a) have trouble remembering what happened (b) really believe the story (c) make up the story as she goes along

Vocabulary Review

1. An *edgy* person is a (a) thin person (b) nervous person (c) smart person
2. A *lavender splotch* on a tablecloth might be caused by (a) red wine (b) beef gravy (c) a very hot serving dish
3. If a right fielder makes a *futile* run for a fly ball, we know that the ball (a) was caught (b) may have been caught (c) was not caught
4. Sometimes letters are returned to the person who sent them stamped DECEASED. This means that the person the letter was sent to has (a) died (b) moved (c) refused delivery
5. An *incredible* story is always (a) exciting (b) untrue (c) hard to believe

Critical Thinking

1. The grandmother mentions "proof" of the ghost. If the story really happened as she said it did, think of at least two "proofs" she might have offered.

2. This story has been told many, many times. Dr. Louis C. Jones of the New York State Historical Society has found more than 75 versions (retellings). Sometimes it goes by other titles, such as "Lavender" or "The Ghostly Hitchhiker." Certain things remain the same in all versions: the ride given to the girl, her disappearance, and the interview with the parents. But other details change. Sometimes the girl is picked up by college boys. Sometimes the sweater is a coat, or is simply left out of the story. Different versions

87

exist, of course, because each new teller thinks he or she can add to the story. Suppose *you* were telling the story. What changes would you make? Why?

3.   Some "true" tall tales never seem to die out. This story is one. Another is the "carburetor" story mentioned in the introduction. Usually, stories of this kind are told as happening to "a good friend of mine" or "someone I really trust." Have you heard any stories of this kind? If so, what are they? If not, ask other people till you find a good one.

Haunted New England

Mary Bolté

*Each section of North America has its own haunting
tales. The South has its creaking old mansions and
moss-draped trees. The West has its ghost trains and
the mysterious Bigfoot. But perhaps strangest of all
are the tales of New England. Why? First, New
England is a very old section, and the old is often
mysterious. Second, much of the land is rocky and
unfriendly. The weather can be cruel. A hard land
produces a hard life. Black magic, evil curses,
witches, hauntings, tombstone terrors—all are parts
of the tradition.*

*Here are three of New England's best tales.
Read them and wonder.*

Vocabulary Preview

CHAMBERS (CHAME burs) rooms; any enclosed spaces, such as caves
- The tunnel led to large underground *chambers.*

DOCUMENTS (DOK yu ments) original or legal papers
- The Constitution and Declaration of Independence are famous *documents.*

JAUNTY (JAWN tee) carefree and happy; bouncy
- A *jaunty* person is usually fun to be with.

RESUSCITATION (ri SUS uh TAY shun) the process of bringing something back to life
- The story was about the *resuscitation* of a corpse.

SORCERY (SORE sur ee) unnatural power over others; black magic
- Witches and wizards are supposed to practice *sorcery.*

WHEEZING (WHEE zing) breathing with a rattling or whistling sound
- Bob's *wheezing* in his sleep bothers me.

WRETCH (RECH) a very unhappy and *wretch*ed person
- The poor *wretch* lives in a shack and has little to eat.

The Ghastly Leg

Colonel Jonathan Buck was the founder of Bucksport, Maine. For years he was the local judge. He was a strict, stern, and stubborn man.

At the end of the 1800s, Buck was faced with a truly awful case. The body of an unknown woman was found. It was in pieces. Missing was one leg that had been chopped off at the knee.

At first there were absolutely no suspects. But it was Colonel Buck's duty to produce a murderer quickly. A local half-wit became his choice. This poor man lived alone in a shack on the edge of town. Some said he had powers of sorcery. He made no effort to obey the rules of society. He lived in a very odd way.

All these things, as far as Buck was concerned, decided the case. The poor wretch was sentenced to death. The day of the hanging arrived. But before the rope was tightened, the doomed man called out to Buck. "The leg! The leg! Mark my words, it will follow you to your grave."

It was not too strange for a man about to hang to damn those who had ordered it. But this case was somehow different. There were many in Bucksport who were glad they weren't in the judge's shoes.

The years passed. The curse was all but forgotten. At last the judge died, still thought by all to be the town's greatest citizen. He was buried with honor. A splendid monument of the finest stone was placed over his grave. But not a day had passed when a strange stain appeared on the stone.

Curious people gathered around. They were amazed. Why, the stain was just the shape of a woman's leg! Old thoughts of the hanged man's curse came back in a flash.

Colonel Buck's family were very angry. They thought the odd mark was the work of a joker. Right away, they sent some workmen to scrub down the monument. Soon it was as smooth and perfect as before. But again the mark appeared, even darker. More cleanings were useless. The stain of the leg is still sharp and distinct. You can see it just below the Colonel's name on the stone. It still reminds people of the guilt of Jonathan Buck.

Captain Chase

Captain Kidd is probably the best known pirate of all time. He was clever. He was cruel. Countless are the places in which Kidd is thought to have buried gold. Just as common are old yellowed maps. These cracked maps are offered as real documents. They tell treasure seekers where to look for hidden gold.

Jewell Island, off the coast of Maine, is a favorite hunting ground. Here greedy people have come for years. They have tried all kinds of ways of finding the gold. But all with no luck. Today many doubt that there is gold buried there at all.

However, one odd story goes on. In the late 1800s, a bony, weatherbeaten traveler arrived at Jewell. He was thought to be strange but harmless. He wore a gold ring in one ear. On his head was a tall stovepipe hat. He carried an accordion strapped to his back. From his shoulder hung a string bag. In it was a map as creased and brown as his face.

The stranger's name, he said, was Willows. The map was the clue to Kidd's lost treasure. All he needed now, he said, was a good compass. And the only man on the island who owned one was Captain Frederick Chase.

Chase was not a completely honest man. In fact, he was something of a pirate himself. He quickly took Willows up on an offer to look for the loot together. He even believed Willows' story about the accordion. The instrument, Willows said, would be of help in the task. Sooner or later, Willows explained, they would get to the right spot. At that point the accordion would sound a long low note. The note would go on till the earth was dug up.

The two men went off into the woods together. From time to time people could hear the accordion. The noises came from all parts of the island. They were wheezing whines. Clearly, the gold was not yet found. But about eleven on the second night, a different sound was heard. It was a steady moan. It was thought to indicate success.

In the morning, people were again surprised. A jaunty Captain Chase left on what looked like a long sea voyage. Soon a search was on for the absent Willows. Things looked suspicious. The searchers did find a freshly dug pit. They also found the track of a heavy object dragged through the sand to the water's edge. But they never found Willows.

Years passed. Chase returned from his trip a rich man. He grew respected. His fine house on the island was a show-place. When he died, he was buried in his own splendid garden. There he might have remained in peace but for a berry picker's luck.

One day this berry picker passed near the old pirate pit. A bad storm had come up. It grew worse. Trees were pulled up by the roots. Parts of a nearby cliff were washed away. Now the berry picker could see a cave for the first time. Entering, he came upon a skeleton. A gold earring still clung to a piece of leathery ear. A stovepipe hat tipped over the skull. All signs seemed to lead to Captain Chase.

Before long, Chase's big house was searched. In fact, it was nearly torn apart. Many hidden chambers were found, and secret passageways. One of them was a damp, dark tunnel. It led to an underground cell. Here were the long-lost treasure map and the dusty old accordion.

It was too late, of course, to try the captain. But the people of the island found their own kind of justice. They took Willows' skeleton from the cave. They buried him with his accordion, next to the captain. There, a ghostly wheezing whine might forever disturb the captain's peace.

Had the treasure really been found by Chase? Most people thought it had. But if so, it was lost once more. Perhaps it now lies hidden deep beneath the ruins of the captain's house.

Frozen Citizens

New England has many strange stories. One of the oddest is about the freezing of old or ill people. This was done, it is said, during the winter months. In that way, the young and the healthy were sure to get enough of the short food supply.

Don't laugh! Not yet. In 1939, a Vermont newspaper

printed an account of this practice. The author was not named. He or she got the story from a grandfather. It happened one January in the 1800s. The grandfather was there when six people, drugged and naked, were taken from a cabin. They were dragged out into the bitter cold. Then they were left overnight in the snow.

This ceremony was held with great calmness. The people even joked as they worked. Afterward, they returned to the cabin. Then came a night of easy sleep.

In the morning, first came a hearty breakfast. Next, the group asked the visitor to watch the rest of the ceremony. The lifeless bodies were now partly covered by fresh snow. They were put into a ten-foot box. They were padded with straw and cloth. Boards were nailed over the top. (For protection against wolves, the article said.) Finally, the box was covered with evergreen branches. All this was done in a casual, regular way. The people seemed to think nothing of it. The visitor was asked to come again the next spring. If he wished, he could watch the resuscitation. The frozen persons would be needed for the planting of corn.

In May the visitor returned. Some snow was still on the ground. He watched as the bodies were taken from the box. They seemed as stiff as before. Then large tubs were filled with warm water. The bodies were added, heads slightly raised. More hot water went into the tubs. Soon color began to return to the cheeks. When breathing began, small amounts of liquor were given. This was followed by a hot meal in the cabin. After eating, all six seemed lively and talkative. They were quite rested after their four-month sleep. They were ready for the spring planting.

As far as is known, this strange practice has not continued to the present day. But many old Vermonters might still welcome such an escape from their long, hard winters.

Recall

1. In "The Ghastly Leg," (a) a judge is punished during his lifetime for an evil act (b) the curse of a man about to die seems to come true (c) a dead woman returns to name her own murderer
2. A magical object in "Captain Chase" is (a) a stovepipe hat (b) an earring (c) an accordion
3. When Willows' skeleton was found, the people of Jewell Island (a) tore Captain Chase's house apart (b) looked for gold in the cave (c) feared the ghost of Captain Chase
4. In "Frozen Citizens," the most amazing thing is that (a) people in the old days sometimes didn't have enough food (b) the old people were killed (c) the old people were brought back to life
5. You could see one of the objects mentioned in the stories if you visited a (a) cemetery in Bucksport, Maine (b) theater in Jewell Island, Maine (c) ten-foot box in a Vermont museum

Infer

6. The story that seems hardest to believe certainly is (a) "The Ghastly Leg" (b) "Captain Chase" (c) "Frozen Citizens"
7. In "The Ghastly Leg," Buck sentenced the half-wit to die because (a) he wanted the case settled (b) he had proof of his guilt (c) the unfortunate man had confessed
8. In "Captain Chase," the author suggests that most old maps of hidden treasure are (a) real documents (b) rare (c) of little value

96

9. Of least importance in proving Captain Chase's guilt was the (a) earring still in the ear (b) fact that Chase got rich (c) accordion and map found under Chase's house
10. In truth, the author of "Frozen Citizens" probably (a) really believes the story (b) is kidding the reader about its truth (c) will try the experiment herself sometime

Vocabulary Review

1. The valuable *document* was finally found in the king's sleeping *chamber.* In other words, (a) the paper was found in the king's closet (b) the original paper was found in the king's bedroom (c) the pig was found in the king's pajamas
2. Witch doctors are said to practice (a) *wheezing* (b) *resuscitation* (c) *sorcery*
3. A *jaunty* person could not be (a) wretched (b) red haired (c) athletic
4. A noise of some kind is always connected with the word (a) *jaunty* (b) *wheezing* (c) *document*
5. A *wretch* is unlikely to be (a) poor (b) hungry (c) rich

Critical Thinking

1. The story of Judge Buck's tombstone, of course, has a natural explanation. What is it? If you don't know, ask a science teacher.
2. By itself, the story of the tombstone seems highly unlikely. But consider this: there are millions and millions of

tombstones in North America. Is it strange that just *once* something like this should happen? One chance in millions? *Perhaps what's really strange is that more strange things don't happen!* Explain this statement. Do you agree?

3. "Captain Chase" contains only one supernatural object. What is it? Do you think the story would be better without it? Why or why not?

4. The author calls persons who search for buried treasure "greedy people." Do you agree, in all cases? When are they greedy? When are they not?

5. The live people in "Frozen Citizens" are described as being calm and even happy at their work. Yet strangely, this idea of happiness *adds* to the horror of the story. Explain why.

6. The author makes it clear that the tale of the frozen people comes from a newspaper. How does this help the story?

7. "Frozen Citizens" is of course quite untrue. Yet it does lead us to think about some true things. For instance, ages and ages ago, useless people *were* often simply left alone to die. And today, if you have enough money, you can arrange to have your body frozen forever when you die. Persons who do this hope that in the future doctors will discover methods of resuscitation and cures for present diseases. If you had the money, would you be interested? Why, or why not?

8. Which of the three stories do you think is the best? Explain why. Give exact reasons, not statements like "more interesting."

In a Dim Room

Lord Dunsany

*Here's a real problem. You're walking alone in the
wilds of India. A tiger starts following you. You
have no gun. You enter a cave. The tiger follows.
The cave goes on . . . and on . . . and on. Behind
you, the tiger gets nearer . . . and nearer . . . and
nearer. Suddenly you come to a blank wall. It's the
end of the cave. How do you escape?*

*An impossible problem? Not at all. Read how a
master storyteller solves it in a surprisingly simple
way.*

Vocabulary Preview

CREDULOUS (KREJ uh lus) too ready to believe; easily fooled
- A *credulous* person will believe almost anything.

DISASTER (di ZAS ter) a truly terrible event
- The plane crashed, and 117 people were killed in the *disaster.*

GAME (GAME) animals or birds that are hunted
- Years ago, rich people used to hunt big *game* in Africa.

INTENTLY (in TENT lee) in a serious, thoughtful, careful manner
- "Now listen *intently,*" said the teacher, "and you'll understand."

LEISURELY (LEE zhur lee) in a relaxed, calm manner
- When the baseball cleared the fence, Laura ran *leisurely* around the bases.

I T IS SOME TIME NOW SINCE I HAVE WRITTEN about my friend Jorkens. The reason is this. I caused a certain amount of trouble in one house by bringing him into it. It was not my fault. Nor do I think it was his.

What happened was quite simple. A friend of mine had said that his children liked thrilling tales. So I told them a few stories about lions and tigers. These quite failed to thrill them. Then I thought of Jorkens. He had unusual stories of adventures with animals in Asia and Africa. Those I had told had failed. But his might be likely to succeed. I told my friend's three children about him. I said that I knew an old hunter of big game. His stories were more out-of-the-way than mine. I asked my friend if I might bring him one day.

I had no idea that there would be anything frightening about one of Jorkens' tales. Nor did I think that the children would be easily frightened. They were, after all, between 10 and 12 years old. The permission to bring Jorkens was given, and the children unfortunately asked for a thrilling tale. They used those actual words. Jorkens began at once, as soon as they asked him. Now it is all blamed on me. I can only say this. They asked for it, and they got it.

It should be kept in mind that they had never seen Jorkens before. They had only his word for what kind of man he was. And then, children can be very credulous. Well, here is the story. He told it almost as soon as he was seated in a comfortable chair. The children stood before him. There were two boys of 10 and 11 and a girl of 12.

It was all about a tiger. But I was counting on his telling a straight story. I had often heard him tell stories to grown-ups. I did not expect him to change his style to suit his audience—if "suit" can be the proper word for the trouble he created.

"The tiger," said Jorkens, "had spotted me. It was following me quite leisurely. Perhaps it did not want to run in the hot weather, and knew perfectly well that I couldn't. My story may serve as a warning to you. When you grow up, never go near an Indian jungle without a gun. Never think that just for once, and for only a short walk, it won't matter. It mattered more than you can possibly guess. For there was the tiger. He was coming slowly after me. I was walking away, and the tiger was walking a little faster than I was. Well, of course I realized my chances. I thought he was only doing five yards in a hundred faster. Even so, I had no chance of escaping by walking. Running would only make it worse."

"Why?" asked the children.

"Why," said Jorkens, "because running would be a new game. The tiger would play it too. At walking he was only gaining five yards in a hundred. But at running he would have gained fifty. That's why I chose walking. Of course, it wasn't any better really. It would end the same way. And it wasn't actually in the jungle. It was on some rocky land outside it. There was no chance of a tree, because I was walking away from the jungle."

"Why?" asked another child.

"Because the tiger was between me and it," said Jorkens. "The tigers go outside the jungle at night. They go back in the very early morning. That's when the birds are waking and screaming. All this was in the early morning. But the sun was well up. I thought that the tigers would all have been back long before. So I went for that walk without a gun. Of course, I was quite mistaken."

"Why were you taking the walk?" asked the girl.

"You should never ask anyone *why* he did anything that leads to disaster," said Jorkens. "All such things are done for the same reason. And that reason a person does not like to admit. But there it is. They are all done for the same reason. Pure foolishness."

"Did it lead to disaster?" asked she.

"You shall hear," said Jorkens. "Well, I told you I was on rocky land. It was hilly too. As I said, the tiger was getting nearer. Right then I saw a cave in the rocks. It was near the top of a little hill. Of course, to go in there would cut off my retreat. But my retreat was doing me no good. And there was nowhere better to go. It seemed to me that the small cave might get smaller. At the end, there might be no room for the tiger. Or it might get larger. In that case, there might be places where I could get away from him. There were just two small hopes and nowhere else to go. So I bent over and went into the cave. Soon the tiger came in too.

"He was still some way behind me. I saw the light go out as he entered, for he filled the entrance. The cave did get smaller. Soon I was on all fours. Still the tiger did not hurry. The cave might get even smaller. Then I might be able to squeeze on where the tiger could not. And it did get a little smaller, but not small enough. We went on over the smooth gray stone. It got darker as we went. After a while I could no longer see the color of the floor. The tiger seemed to soak up all the daylight.

"A faint hope came to me then. I thought of a story about the skeleton of a mouse. It had been found in a wall of a church. Just behind it was the skeleton of a cat. It had got where the cat could not follow, but it didn't do much good. I hoped that the tiger would have more sense than that cat. But still the cave ran on. And still the tiger wasn't hurrying. That seemed to make my chances even worse. That tiger was so sure. Of course I could smell him behind me, for he was still gaining. But the smell seemed almost too strong for a tiger thirty yards behind. An awful thought came to me. This cave might be the tiger's own home. That is very much what it seemed to me.

"Then came another hope. It came after going some

distance. I wondered if the cave might soon come out through the little hill. What good that would have done me, I don't quite know. Still, silly as it may seem, that was what I wanted. There I was, going on all fours. For the tiger, that sort of walking was natural. It seemed better to lose ground slowly walking in the open. For who knew what lay on the other side of the hill? I thought I might find a tree. But there was no draft in my face. There was only the smell of the tiger in the darkness. I realized I would never come to the open air."

I glanced at the children's faces. Was Jorkens holding their attention better that I had done? They were certainly listening intently. But I could not see much more interest than they had shown in my poor story. An idea came to me then. It might have been quite unfair, but it was this. The feelings of the girl, as far as she had any, were on the side of the tiger. Of course, that may have been quite wrong. I should perhaps say that it was in the fall. No lights had yet been turned on. I had no idea what was coming.

"The tiger was gaining rapidly," Jorkens went on. "The floor, as I said, was perfectly smooth. It was quite clear that it must have for long been polished. By what? By soft feet, the large feet of a heavy animal. There were no rough edges anywhere I put my hand. And then the smooth floor came to an end. In front of me was a smooth rock without a crack in it. There was no turn to the left or right. The cave had ended. I turned around in the dark. I smelled, rather than saw, the tiger."

"What happened then?" asked one of the boys.

"He ate me," said Jorkens. "It is a ghost that is speaking to you now."

And then the fuss started in that dim room. It was blamed entirely on me.

Recall

1. Jorkens comes to the children's house to (a) tell them stories (b) see some old friends (c) listen to their strange tales
2. According to Jorkens, tigers usually spend the daytime hours (a) in caves (b) in the open (c) in jungles
3. According to Jorkens, the reason for acts that lead to very bad results is always (a) the hidden urge to punish oneself (b) pure foolishness (c) greed
4. During his time in the cave, Jorkens has (a) fears and hopes (b) only fears (c) only hopes
5. Jorkens comes to believe that the cave is the tiger's home because of the (a) bones lying about on the floor and the smell (b) smooth floor and the bones lying about (c) smell and the smooth floor
6. The shock at the end is that (a) the tiger smiles (b) Jorkens is eaten (c) the tiger is really a man dressed up in an animal costume

Infer

7. The story of the mouse and the cat in the church wall shows that (a) an escape can turn into a trap (b) mice are smarter than cats (c) cats are smarter than mice
8. Jorkens' failure to feel a draft on his face indicates to him that the cave has no (a) streams or water falls (b) bats in it (c) second entrance
9. Throughout Jorkens' story of his adventure in the cave, the reader believes that he escaped because (a) he is telling it himself in later years (b) the author has told us this earlier (c) tigers are not really as dangerous as the story would have us believe

10. The author's main purpose in writing the story was to (a) encourage his readers to carry guns (b) show how to escape from tigers (c) surprise the reader with a clever twist at the end

Vocabulary Review

On your paper, write the choice in parentheses that makes the most sense.

1. Taking a driver's test for the first time, you would probably drive rather (intently, leisurely).
2. The term *"game* birds" probably means birds that are (playful, hunted).
3. A *credulous* person is easily (fooled, taught).
4. Driving a car in too leisurely a way can result in (disaster, game).

Critical Thinking

1. Why do you think the author had a character named Jorkens tell the story? Why didn't he just tell it himself?

2. Do you agree that the reason for actions that lead to disaster is always "pure foolishness"? Explain.

3. Is the author correct in thinking he is unfairly blamed for the effects of Jorkens' story? If it led to disaster, was "pure foolishness" in any way a cause?

4. What does the author mean by stating that the "feelings of the girl, as far as she had any, were on the side of the tiger"? Why might the girl feel this way?

5. How did you think the story was going to end? Suppose the last two paragraphs were left off. (Look back.) Would you have guessed the ending? How else might the story end? Remember, your ending must be interesting to the children.

The Faithful Ghost

Jerome K. Jerome

*Do you believe in ghosts? Do most people? Perhaps it
doesn't really matter. Someone once said that the real
question is this: Do ghosts believe in people?*

*Old Johnson, the ghost in this story, certainly
believed in people. He loved one in particular. He
was faithful to a long-lost love named Emily. He
haunted her house for years.*

*But finally Johnson got to be too much of a
nuisance. He had to be got rid of. Just how was this
done? Well, it's quite a story. . . .*

Vocabulary Preview

AGENT (AY junt) a person who acts for another
- We never saw the house's owner because we rented in through an *agent.*

BLISSFUL (BLIS ful) very happy; full of joy
- Ms. Bright's vacation was two *blissful* weeks in the mountains.

BYGONE (BY gon) gone by; past
- Old Mr. Naughts lived with memories of *bygone* times.

CEREMONY (SER uh mo nee) very polite conduct
- At my aunt's house meals are eaten with a lot of *ceremony.*

UNDETECTED (un dee TEK ted) not found out or discovered
- The gas leak went *undetected* until the explosion.

UTTERED (UT urd) spoken; given out
- Emilio *uttered* a cry of pain.

I

WAS ONLY A BOY WHEN I FIRST MET WITH
Johnson. I was home for the Christmas holidays. It was
Christmas Eve. I had been allowed to sit up very late. Finally
it was *too* late. I opened the door of my little bedroom to go
in—and I found myself face to face with Johnson.

Johnson was coming out of the bedroom. It passed
through me. It uttered a long, low, sad cry. Then it disappeared out the stairway window.

I was shocked for a moment. I was only a schoolboy at
the time. I had never seen a ghost before. Going to bed that
night made me nervous. But I thought for a little while. It
was only sinful people that ghosts could harm. So I got into
bed, and I went to sleep.

In the morning I told my father what I had seen.

"Oh, yes, that was old Johnson," he answered. "Don't
you be frightened of that. It lives here." And then he told
me the poor thing's history.

It was a sad tale. It seemed that Johnson, now a ghost,
had once been very much alive. He had loved, in early life,
the daughter of a former owner of our house. She was a very
beautiful girl. Her first name had been Emily. Father did not
know her other name.

Johnson was too poor to marry the girl. So he kissed her
goodbye. He told her he would soon be back. Then he went
off to Australia to make his fortune.

But Australia was not then what it is now and Johnson
could find no work. He became a robber. But travelers were
few and far between. Even when Johnson could catch one
alone, there was likely to be little of value. Sometimes there
was nothing. And he couldn't always work undetected.
There were the police and the judges to pay off. It was not

an easy life for Johnson. It took him nearly twenty years to make his fortune.

But the job was at last done. He managed to fool the police. He got out of Australia. He then returned to England, full of hope and joy, to claim his bride.

Finally he reached Emily's house. It was silent and dark. The neighbors could tell him little. Soon after he had left, Emily's family had, one foggy night, quietly disappeared. Nobody had seen anything of them since. Nobody had heard anything. It was all very strange. Their landlord had looked hard for them. So had many people who ran local stores.

Poor Johnson was crazy with sadness. He looked for his lost love all over the world. But he never found her. Finally he did the best thing possible. He returned to the very house Emily had lived in. There, he said, he would end his lonely life. It was a house of memories. He thought only of the happy bygone days. No, she was not still there. But this was the very house where he and his beloved Emily had passed so many blissful hours.

He had lived there quite alone. He wandered about the empty rooms. He often broke down weeping. He called to his Emily to come back to him. This went on for years. And when poor old Johnson died, his ghost still kept on doing the same thing.

It was just that way, Father said, when he rented the house. The renting agent knew about it. He had knocked a pile of money off the rent. Who would want to live in a house with a ghost?

That Christmas holiday, as I have said, provided my first meeting with Johnson. After that, I kept on meeting it. I met it about the place at all times of the night. And so, indeed, did we all. Sometimes we walked around it. At other times, we stood aside to let it pass. But soon we grew more at home with it. There seemed to be no reason for so much ceremony. We got used to walking straight through it. You could not say it was ever much in our way.

It was a gentle, harmless old ghost. We all felt very sorry for it. We even pitied it. Some people, indeed, made quite a pet of it. Its faithfulness touched them so.

But time went on, and things changed. The ghost grew to be a bit of a bore. You could see it was full of sadness. There was nothing cheerful or happy about it. You felt very sorry for it. But still, it got on your nerves. It would sit on the stairs and cry for hours at a time. We would hear it when we woke up in the night. It would be in the hall. Or it would be going in and out of different rooms. Always, it would be moaning and sighing. We could not get to sleep again easily.

The ghost was worst when we had a party. It would sit outside the living room door. It would cry all the time. It didn't do anybody any harm, exactly. But it made everything that was going on very sad.

"Oh, I'm getting sick of that old fool," said my father one day. Johnson had just been more of a nuisance than usual. He had spoiled a game of cards. He had sat up in the chimney, groaning and moaning.

"We really have to get rid of him," said my father. "Somehow or other, we really do. I wish I knew how to do it."

"Well," said my mother, "you know this much. You'll never see the end of him till he's found Emily's grave. That's what he's after. You have to find Emily's grave. Show him where it is. And then he'll stop haunting us. That's the only thing to do."

The idea seemed like a good one. But there was one trouble with it. No one knew where Emily's grave was. No one knew any more about it than Johnson did. Father suggested looking around for a grave that had *Emily* on it. But luck wasn't with him. There was no other Emily buried for miles around. I never saw such a neighborhood. No *Emilys* at all!

I thought for a bit. Then I made a suggestion myself.

"Couldn't we fake something? I asked. "Johnson seems to be a simple-minded old ghost. He might be fooled. Anyhow, we could try it."

"That's it! So we will!" cried my father. And the very next morning he called some workers in. They fixed up a little grave at the bottom of the lawn. It had a tombstone over it. And on the stone were the words:

SACRED
To the Memory of
EMILY

Her Last Words Were:
"Tell Johnson I Love Him"

"That ought to get him," said Dad. We stood looking at the tombstone when finished. "And I sure hope it does."

It did.

Johnson went down there that very night. And—well— it was one of the saddest things I've ever seen. Johnson jumped upon the tombstone and cried. Dad and the rest of us cried like babies when we saw it.

Johnson has never troubled us since then. Every night is spent sobbing on the grave. Things seem quite happy.

More still? Oh, yes. I'll take you people down and show you. Just come around when Johnson comes to our place— 10:00 P.M. to 4:00 A.M. are the general hours. But 10:00 P.M. to 2:00 A.M. on weekends.

Recall

1. Johnson moved into the house to (a) find Emily's ghost (b) live with memories of Emily (c) scare the people
2. When Johnson died, (a) Emily returned (b) his body was never buried (c) he became a sad ghost
3. The family decides to get rid of Johnson because (a) it is scaring them (b) they want to sell the house (c) it is causing too much trouble
4. The plan to fool the ghost is thought of by (a) the boy (b) the father (c) the mother
5. At the end of the story, old Johnson believes that (a) Emily died loving him (b) Emily is still alive (c) Emily's ghost can be seen by everyone
6. Johnson's activities in Australia seem to have been (a) done with Emily's help (b) useful to that country (c) illegal

Infer

7. The narrator seems to have gone to (a) Australia (b) an English boarding school (c) a French college
8. When Emily's family moved away, they left (a) all their furniture (b) unpaid bills (c) a ghost behind
9. Although a ghost, Johnson could (a) be seen in a mirror (b) read (c) pass over water
10. The narrator's invitation to show the reader Emily's grave (a) proves his greed (b) is made to help Johnson (c) is made as a joke

113

Vocabulary Review

1. A person who always acts with *ceremony* (a) likes large groups of people (b) is very polite (c) is somehow like a ghost

2. The term *"blissful, bygone* days" means (a) happy times of old (b) peaceful periods with no wars (c) days filled with travel

3. Smoke that is *undetected* is (a) harmless (b) black (c) unnoticed

4. An actor's *agent* probably (a) helps with makeup (b) tries to get jobs for the actor (c) sells and rents houses

5. If you *utter* something, you (a) throw it out (b) get tired of it (c) say it

Critical Thinking

1. In one important way, Johnson is different from most other ghosts in stories. What is this way? How does it add to the story?

2. Near the end of the story is an odd combination of sentences: "Every night is spent sobbing on the grave. Things seem quite happy." Explain in your own words how Johnson can be *sobbing* and *happy* at the same time.

3. In most of the story, the ghost is referred to as *it.* But at the end, the ghost is called "he." This is probably no accident. (Jerome K. Jerome was a skilled, careful writer.) Why do you think the author made the change?

4. There is another story very much like "The Faithful Ghost." It is John Kendrick Bangs' "The Water Ghost of Harrowby Hall." Find it if you can. (It has been reprinted in many books, including Globe Book Company's *Tales of Mystery and the Unknown.*) How is it like, and unlike "The Faithful Ghost"?

The House

André Maurois

Ghost stories are as old as history. Thousands of them have been written over the years. You'd think that every possible ghost story had already been told. But no! Authors are still coming up with new ideas. You've probably never read a story quite like "The House."

"The House" is a modern story by a famous French writer. It's told in an odd fashion. The author puts his tale in the mouth of a mysterious woman. We know little about her. She lives in Paris, the capital of France. But beyond that, we learn almost nothing. Her age, her name, her job, her appearance—all are hidden. In a way, this makes her story even more strange.

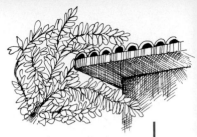

Vocabulary Preview

CHATEAU (sha TOE) a large, expensive country house (from the French)
- The skiers stayed at a *chateau* in the mountains.

GROVE (GROVE) a group of trees
- The park contained a *grove* of pine trees.

LINDEN (LIN dun) a kind of tree often planted for shade
- *Linden* trees have large, heart-shaped leaves.

OUTSKIRTS (OWT skurts) suburbs; the area around a city
- Penny grew up in the *outskirts* of Toronto.

PHANTOM (FAN tum) ghost; apparition; illusion
- A ghost is a *phantom* that some people believe they have seen.

POPLAR (POP lur) a kind of tall, fast-growing tree
- A row of *poplar* trees faced the house.

SLATE (SLATE) a kind of rock that splits into thin layers.
- Long ago roofs and blackboards were often made of *slate.*

TWO YEARS AGO," SHE SAID, "I WAS VERY sick. I realized that I was dreaming the same dream night after night. I was walking in the country. In the distance, I could see a white house. It was long and low, surrounded by a grove of linden trees. To the left of the house was a field and some tall poplar trees. The tops of the poplars could be seen from far off. They were swaying above the lindens.

"In my dream, I was drawn to this house. I walked toward it. A white wooden gate closed the entrance. I opened it. Then I walked along a graceful, curving path. The path was lined by trees. Under them I found spring flowers that faded the moment I picked them. At the end of the path, I was only a few steps from the house. In front of it, there was a great green lawn. It was clipped bare, like the English lawns. A single bed of violet flowers surrounded it.

"The house was built of white stone. It had a slate roof. The door—a heavy wooden door—was at the top of some steps. I wanted to visit the house. But no one answered when I called. I was very, very disappointed. I rang and rang. I shouted—and finally I woke up.

"That was my dream. For months it kept coming back. Each time it was exactly the same, in every detail. Finally I thought: Surely I must have seen this house as a child. I must have played on this lawn. But I could never find the place again in my memory. Neither could I forget the idea that I must have seen it. More and more, that idea filled my thoughts. At last I knew what I must do. I'd learned to drive a little car. I decided to spend my vacation driving through France. I'd search all summer for my dream house.

"I'm not going to tell you about my travels. I explored

117

the North, the West, the South. I found nothing, which didn't really surprise me. In October I came back to Paris. All winter long I continued to dream about the white house. Last spring I went back to my old habit of making trips to the outskirts of Paris. One day I was crossing a valley near l'Isle-Adam. Suddenly I felt a pleasant shock. It was a strange feeling. A very strange feeling! Like suddenly recognizing people or places you have loved in the past.

"I had never been in that particular valley before. But I was perfectly at home in it! On my right were the tops of some poplars. They stood out above a grove of linden trees. Through the leaves I could see the house. Then I knew that I had found it! This was my dream chateau! I knew what I would find a hundred yards ahead. There would be a narrow road cutting across the highway. The road was there. I followed it. It led me to a white gate.

"There began the path I had so often followed. Under the trees were the same spring flowers. Then I came to the great green lawn. I saw the little flight of steps. At the top was the huge wooden door. Moving quickly, I ran up the steps and rang the bell.

"I was worried. I was afraid no one would answer. But almost at once, a servant appeared. It was a man. He had a sad face, very old. He was wearing a black jacket. Oddly, he seemed very surprised to see me. He looked at me closely without saying a word.

" 'I'm going to ask you a favor,' I said. 'A rather strange favor. I don't know the owners of this house. But I'd be very happy if they'd let me visit it.'

" 'The chateau is for rent, Madame,' he said. His voice seemed somehow sad. 'And I am here to show it.'

" 'For rent?' I exclaimed. 'What luck! It's too much to

have hoped for. But the house is so beautiful! Why aren't the owners living in it?'

" 'The owners did live in it, Madame. They moved out when it became haunted.'

" 'Haunted?' I said. 'That will scarcely stop me. I didn't know people in France still believed in ghosts. Even people in the country.'

" 'I am forced to believe in them, Madame,' he said seriously. 'You see, I myself have met, on the path at night, the same phantom that drove the owners away.'

" 'What a story!' I said, trying to smile.

" 'It is not a story, Madam,' the old man said. He gave me a stern look. 'And you least of all should laugh at it. For you see, the phantom was you.' "

Recall

1. The dreams of the narrator (the person who tells the story) began (a) during a period of illness (b) after she had seen the house (c) while she was reading ghost stories
2. According to the narrator, the dream of the house (a) was repeated two or three times each night (b) always led to a happy ending (c) was always exactly the same
3. The narrator finally finds the house (a) in the northern part of France (b) in the country near Paris (c) on an island in the sea
4. The narrator is surprised to learn that the house is (a) filled with phantoms (b) for rent because of a ghost in the area (c) empty of all furniture

5. At the end of the story, we learn that the ghost is (a) a long-dead owner (b) a servant (c) the narrator herself

Infer

6. Throughout the story, the narrator seems (a) in perfect control of her actions (b) rather unable to help herself (c) about to die of worry
7. In the dream, the narrator's ringing at the door never produced any results. This was probably because (a) people inside thought a ghost was at the door (b) no one was home (c) the bell was out of order
8. After reading the story, we still don't know much about the narrator. But we can infer certain things about her. Which of the following descriptions might best fit her? (a) About 75, very rich, and in poor health throughout the story (b) About 30, with a good job and more than enough money (c) About 20, unemployed but hopeful
9. The author's purpose in providing so little information about the narrator was probably to (a) shorten the story for easy reading (b) make her seem more like a mysterious phantom (c) make the reader angry
10. The introduction spoke of the story's containing a "new idea." This idea is that (a) ghosts prefer large old houses (b) some people have been driven from their homes by ghosts (c) the self in a dream can haunt someone in real life

Vocabulary Review

1. If you saw a *phantom* in a *grove,* you saw (a) a car in a field (b) a ghost among some trees (c) a ghost in a grave

2. A *chateau* in the *outskirts* might accurately be called (a) a cat in a pants suit (b) a castle near Paris (c) a large house in the suburbs

3. Before paper became common, children in school wrote on *slates*, or (a) sheets of hard black rock (b) paper bags (c) skins of animals

4. A large building in the Bronx is called "Linden House." In front of it, you might expect to see (a) old people in wheelchairs (b) used cars for sale (c) a large shade tree

5. *Poplars* are (a) hit records (b) trees (c) popcorn candy bars

Critical Thinking

1. Good authors often say things indirectly. In other words, they give certain facts from which the reader makes inferences. In "The House," the person who answers the door is called only a "servant." But exactly what kind of servant is he? Think about the way he is dressed and the way he talks. Then decide who or what he might be.

2. Explain in your own words why, although no one came to the door in the dream, someone did answer the bell in real life.

3. In your opinion, just how possible is the story? What would a person have to believe to think that the story could really happen?

4. Nearly all people have dreams that keep coming back. Do you? If you do, try to do just what the author of "The House" did. Think of some way that the dream, or part of it, suddenly becomes part of your real life. Invent some more details, some more surprises. For instance, a person in your dream might have your real life as part of his or her dream. Finally, write or tell the whole story.

5. The famous American author Mark Twain has an interesting story about a repeated dream. It's called "My Platonic Sweetheart." Find it in a library and report to the class.

6. "The House" illustrates two rules for quotation marks that you may not know. Look at the way quotes are used in most of the paragraphs. Look at the way they're used at the end, when the characters are talking to each other. State these two rules in your own words.

The King o' the Cats

Joseph Jacobs

"The King o' the Cats" and the story that follows it
are the two oldest in this book. Both have probably
been told for 500 years. They come from old
England, a land of misty phantoms and savage
spooks.

Cats, of course, have long stalked through
spooky stories. Why? No one knows the whole
answer. But cats do love the cover of darkness. They
like to be alone. They're private. They seem to have
secrets. You've met cats in stories before, but never
one like Old Tom, "The King o' the Cats."

Vocabulary Preview

COFFIN (KOF in) a casket; a box in which a
dead person is buried
   • The *coffin* was carried by six of the
   dead man's friends.

CORONET (KOR uh net) a small crown
   • The princess wore a *coronet* on her
   head.

PALL (POL) a heavy cloth spread over a coffin
   • The purple *pall* was removed before
   the coffin was buried.

SEXTON (SEKS tun) a person who takes care of
a church
   • Long ago a church's *sexton* often
   buried the dead.

SOLEMNLY (SOL um lee) very seriously
   • The dead person's family entered the
   church *solemnly.*

VELVET (VEL vit) a kind of heavy, soft cloth
   • The new stage curtains are made of
   velvet.

ONE WINTER EVENING THE SEXTON'S WIFE was sitting by the fireside. Beside her, on the floor, was her big black cat. Old Tom was half asleep. He was waiting for his master to come home.

They waited and they waited. But still the sexton didn't come. At last he came rushing in, out of breath.

"Who's Tommy Tildrum?" the sexton called out. He spoke in a wild way. Both his wife and his cat stared at him. What was the matter?

"Why, what's the matter?" said his wife. "And why do you want to know who Tommy Tildrum is?"

"Oh, I've had such a time. I was digging away at old Mr. Fordyce's grave. I sat down to rest. I suppose I must have dropped asleep. I woke up hearing a cat's *meow*."

"Meow!" said Old Tom in answer.

"Yes, just like that. So I looked over the edge of the grave. And what do you think I saw?"

"Now, how can I tell?" said the sexton's wife.

"Why, nine black cats! All like our friend Tom here. All with a white spot on their chests. And what do you think they were doing?"

"Well, how can I tell?" said the sexton's wife.

"Carrying a small coffin, they were. A small coffin covered with a black velvet pall. And on the pall was a small coronet, all of gold. And at every third step they took, they all cried out together, *'Meow.'"*

"Meow!" said Old Tom again.

"Yes, just like that," said the sexton. "And they were coming nearer and nearer to me. I could see them more clearly. Their eyes shone out with a sort of green light. Well,

125

they all came toward me. Eight of them were carrying the coffin. And the biggest, he was walking in front. For all the world, he looked like———— But look at our Tom! See how he's looking at me? You'd think he knew all I was saying."

"Go on, go on," said his wife. "Never mind Old Tom."

"Well, as I was saying, they came toward me. They were walking slowly and solemnly. And at every third step they all cried together, *'Meow.'*"

"Meow!" said Old Tom again.

"Yes, just like that. By and by they came and stood right opposite Mr. Fordyce's grave. Then they all stood still. They looked straight at me. I did feel strange, I did. But look at Old Tom! He's looking at me just the way they did!"

"Go on, go on," said his wife. "Never mind Old Tom."

"Now, where was I? Oh, they all stood still, looking at me. Then the one that wasn't carrying the coffin came forward. He stared straight at me. And he said to me—yes, *said* to me—with a squeaky voice, 'Tell Tommy Tildrum that Tim Toldrum's dead! So that's why I asked you who Tom Tildrum was. For how can I tell Tom Tildrum that Tim Toldrum's dead if I don't know who Tom Tildrum is?"

"Look at Old Tom! Look at Old Tom!" screamed his wife.

And well he might look. For Tom was swelling up, and Tom was staring. And at last Tom cried out, "What—Old Tim's dead! That means I'm King o' the Cats!" Then he rushed up the chimney and was nevermore seen.

Recall

1. When the story begins, Old Tom is (a) with his master in the graveyard (b) hunting mice (c) waiting for the sexton to come home

126

2. The sexton tells his odd story as a (a) dream (b) real experience (c) made-up story
3. The sexton has (a) a message for Tommy Tildrum (b) a dead cat (c) white hair from fright
4. At the end of the story, the new King o' the Cats (a) puts on his crown (b) rewards his master (c) disappears up the chimney
5. The cats in the funeral procession all (a) carried the coffin (b) seemed to be working together (c) gave a message to the sexton
6. In the cats' coffin was the body of (a) Tim Toldrum (b) Tom Tildrum (c) Mr. Fordyce

Infer

7. The funeral procession is amusing because (a) the pall is black, not white (b) it is a copy of a human procession (c) the sexton has very bad eyes
8. The royal blood of the dead cat is suggested by (a) a gold coffin (b) the cats' song (c) a small crown
9. Tommy Tildrum turns out to be (a) the sexton's own cat (b) the dead cat (c) the pastor of the church
10. The story suggests that cats (a) will someday take over the earth (b) have mysterious powers unknown to most humans (c) are not as smart as we think they are

Vocabulary Review

On your paper, write the choice in each pair of parentheses that makes the most sense.
1. The *(coffin, coronet)* was covered with a *(sexton, pall)*.
2. The old *(pall, sexton)* dug the grave *(velvet, solemnly)*.
3. In the museum, we saw a silver *(coronet, sexton)* on a *(velvet, coffin)* pillow.

Critical Thinking

1. Why is the sexton the right person to receive the black cats' message?

2. Just for fun, shut your eyes and try to *visualize* (see with your "mind's eye") the scene in the graveyard. Try to see every detail and action. Then try to visualize the end of the story. Which scene do you think is the better? Why?

3. The story mentions several things that are common to many spooky tales. The first of these is indicated by the first three words: the story happens at *night*. Ghostly tales are much more likely to happen at night than in the daytime. See if you can find three other things that are often found in such stories.

4. "The King o' the Cats," of course, is an unbelievable story. Yet most readers can believe it *just enough* to make it enjoyable. There are two reasons for this. The first is that the unbelievable scene in the graveyard is told by a character in the story, not by the author directly. This method of telling a story almost always makes strange events easier to believe. Can you explain why?

The second reason is that cats sometimes actually do things that are hard to believe. Do you know any amazing —*but true*—stories about cats? If so, tell them to the class.

SHOCK WAVES

Those who'll play with cats
must expect to be
scratched.

Miguel de Cervantes

Mr. Fox

Joseph Jacobs

*Now we come to the last of the book's three sections.
It's called "Shock Waves." First we'll meet the
famous and fascinating "Mr. Fox."*

*Someone once said that you can't separate what
happens in a story from the way that it's told. This
is often true. The following old tale proves it.*

*"Mr. Fox" is an odd mixture. It's filled with
horror, and it ends in violence. Yet it's told in a
poetic, sing-song fashion. Somehow, the method of
telling becomes part of the story and lessens the
terror. See if you don't find that this is so. And
remember, "Mr. Fox" is hundreds and hundreds of
years old.*

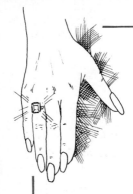

Vocabulary Preview

CHAMBER (CHAME bur) a room; any enclosed area
- The large *chamber* on the third floor was the family's game room.

CONTRACT (KON trakt) a written, legal agreement
- The striking workers wanted a better *contract* with the company.

LEST (LEST) for fear that
- Study hard *lest* you fail the test.

MOAT (MOTE) a deep wide ditch that surrounds a castle
- In time of war, the *moat* around the castle was filled with water.

SUITOR (SOOT ur) a man who is courting a woman with the idea of marriage
- My sister Penny can't decide between two *suitors.*

L ADY MARY WAS YOUNG, AND LADY MARY was fair. She had two brothers. She had more suitors than she could count. But of them all, the bravest and most charming was a Mr. Fox.

Lady Mary had met Mr. Fox at her father's house in the country. No one knew who Mr. Fox was. But he was certainly brave, and surely rich. Of all her suitors, Lady Mary cared for him alone. And at last, what *would* happen did happen. They agreed to be married. Lady Mary asked Mr. Fox where they would live. He described to her his castle. He told her exactly where it was. But, strange to say, he did not ask her or her brothers to come and see it.

The wedding day grew nearer, and nearer still. Lady Mary had not yet seen the castle. One day curiosity got the better of her. Her brothers were out. Mr. Fox was away on a business trip, or so he said. So Lady Mary set out for Mr. Fox's castle. She searched for a long time. At last she came to it, and a fine strong house it was. It had high walls and a deep moat. Soon she was at the gateway. She saw written on it:

BE BOLD, BE BOLD.

But the gate was open. She went through it, and found no one there. So she went up to the doorway. Over it she found written:

BE BOLD, BE BOLD. BUT NOT TOO BOLD.

Still she went on. She walked into a hall. Then she went

133

up some wide stairs. She came to a large wooden door. Over it was written:

> BE BOLD, BE BOLD. BUT NOT TOO BOLD.
> LEST YOUR HEART'S BLOOD SHOULD RUN COLD.

But Lady Mary was a brave one, she was. She opened the door, and what do you think she saw? Why, bodies and skeletons of beautiful young ladies. All were stained with blood. So Lady Mary thought it was high time to get out of that horrid place. She left, closing the door. She went down the stairs. She entered the hall. But then, who should she see through a window but Mr. Fox. He was dragging a beautiful young lady in from the gateway. Then he was at the door. Lady Mary hid herself behind a barrel just in time.

Mr. Fox came in with the poor young lady. She seemed to have fainted. He dragged her down the hall. Soon he was quite near Lady Mary. He stopped suddenly. He had noticed a diamond ring glittering on the finger of the young lady. He tried to pull it off. But it was tightly fixed, and would not come off. So Mr. Fox cursed and swore. He drew his sword and raised it. Then he brought it down upon the hand of the poor lady. The sword cut off the hand, which flew up into the air. It fell, of all places, into Lady Mary's lap. Mr. Fox looked about a bit. But he did not think of looking behind the barrel. So at last he went on, dragging the young lady up the stairs into the Bloody Chamber.

Soon Lady Mary heard the door close after Mr. Fox. She crept out of the castle. She sped through the gateway. She ran home as fast as she could.

Now it happened that the very next day was an important one. The marriage contract was to be signed. There was to be a special breakfast before that. And all went as planned. Mr. Fox sat down at the table opposite Lady Mary. He looked at her sharply.

"How pale you are this morning, my dear," said Mr. Fox.

"Yes," said Lady Mary. "I had a bad night's rest last night. I had horrible dreams."

"Dreams go by opposites," said Mr. Fox. "But tell us your dream. Your sweet voice will make the time pass till the happy hour comes."

"Well," said Lady Mary, "it was like this. I dreamed that I went to your castle. I found it deep in the woods. It had high walls and a deep moat. And over the gateway was written:

BE BOLD, BE BOLD."

"But it is not so, nor was it so," said Mr. Fox.

Lady Mary went on: "And then I came to the doorway. Over it was written:

BE BOLD, BE BOLD. BUT NOT TOO BOLD."

"It is not so, nor was it so," said Mr. Fox.

"Then I went upstairs," Lady Mary continued. "I came to a large wooden door. And over it was written:

BE BOLD, BE BOLD. BUT NOT TOO BOLD.
LEST YOUR HEART'S BLOOD SHOULD RUN COLD."

"It is not so, nor was it so," said Mr. Fox.

"And then—and then I opened the door. The room was filled with bodies and skeletons! Bodies and skeletons of poor dead women. All were stained with blood."

135

"It is not so, nor was it so. And God forbid it should be so," said Mr. Fox.

"Then I rushed downstairs. I saw you coming. You were dragging a young lady by the arm. I had just time to hide behind a barrel. And then you passed me, Mr. Fox. I thought I saw you try to take off her diamond ring. That's the way it seemed in my dream. And when you could not, you took out your sword. You hacked off the poor lady's hand."

"It is not so, nor was it so. And God forbid it should be so," said Mr. Fox. He rose from his seat. He was going to say something else, when Lady Mary cried out:

"But it is so, and it was so. Here's hand and ring I have to show!" At the same time, she pulled out the lady's hand from her dress. She pointed it straight at Mr. Fox.

At once her brothers and her friends drew their swords. They cut Mr. Fox into a thousand pieces.

Recall

1. Lady Mary agrees to marry Mr. Fox because he is (a) stronger than the other suitors (b) from a well-known family (c) brave, charming, and rich .

2. Lady Mary finds it strange that Mr. Fox does not (a) ever leave her side (b) invite her to his castle (c) speak in a charming way

3. Once in the castle, Lady Mary finds (a) ghosts of Mr. Fox's dead wives (b) bodies of beautiful ladies (c) riches beyond belief

4. Lady Mary tells her experience to Mr. Fox (a) as a dream (b) with many changes (c) leaving him entirely out of the story

5. At the end of the story, Lady Mary (a) uses a sword on Mr. Fox (b) forgives Mr. Fox (c) points a dead hand at Mr. Fox

Infer

6. Early in the story is this sentence: "No one knew who Mr. Fox was." This means that no one (a) knew his name (b) knew his family and background (c) was acquainted with Mr. Fox
7. If the marriage had taken place as planned, Lady Mary probably would have (a) been killed (b) continued to live with her brothers (c) enjoyed life in the castle
8. "Mr. Fox" is a good name because it (a) indicates that the story is really about animals (b) contains the lucky combination of three letters (c) suggests trickery
9. Little in the story indicates that Lady Mary was (a) curious, young, and popular (b) headstrong, dumb, and demanding (c) brave, young, and beautiful
10. The story suggests that even hundreds of years ago some women were thought of as (a) people who loved to be ordered about (b) murderers (c) brave and clever

Vocabulary Review

Write on your paper the word in *italics* that belongs in each blank on page 138.

chamber	*lest*	*suitor*
contract	*moat*	

1. The castle was surrounded by a deep _____.
2. Can you imagine that your father was once your mother's _____?
3. Dad signed a _____ to buy a new car yesterday.
4. Many old houses have a _____ called a parlor.
5. Wear a raincoat and boots _____ you catch a cold.

Critical Thinking

1. Why do you think that "Mr. Fox" has been a popular story for hundreds of years? (Think about the picture it paints of women and men. Think too about hidden fears and suspicions that some readers might have.)

2. Many old stories also make use of *stock characters.* These are characters the reader has already met in other stories under different names: the cruel king, the beautiful princess, the selfless knight, for example. Note that both Lady Mary and Mr. Fox are stock characters. We read the first sentence, and we feel we know Lady Mary well. She's the young, popular, wealthy beauty of fairy-tale land. Since we recognize her at once, she does not need to be described in detail. What words are used to describe Mr. Fox? In what ways is he a stock character?

The Story of an Hour

Kate Chopin

*Today authors can write about anything they want.
No subject, however shocking, is forbidden. But not
back in the 1890s! In that age, an important duty of
a writer was to be proper. Certain subjects were
avoided—completely.*

*Then along came writers like Kate Chopin. Her
aim was to present life's truths as she saw them. She
dared to suggest that a wife might not always be
madly in love with her husband. As a result, her
stories were called "shocking," "sinful," and even
"poison." Read this one and you may see why.*

Vocabulary Preview

ABANDONMENT (uh BAN dun ment) the state of having given oneself up to strong inner feelings
- Carlos cried with wild *abandonment* when his mother died.

ELIXIR (i LIK sur) a liquid with amazing, magical powers
- Ponce de Leon searched for the *elixir* of the Fountain of Youth.

INTENTION (in TEN shun) what a person intends, or plans to do
- Marsha's *intention* is to work next summer.

MONSTROUS (MON strus) horrible; like a monster
- To plan a murder is a *monstrous* act.

PIERCING (PEER sing) cutting or stabbing through something
- The *piercing* siren of the police car hurt my ears.

REPRESSION (ri PRESH un) the "bottling up" of inner feelings
- You should not let all your feelings show, but too much *repression* is also bad.

WILL (WIL) the ability to do what you think you should do
- My *will* is not strong enough to make me do my homework tonight.

LOUISE MALLARD, HER FRIENDS KNEW, HAD heart trouble. For this reason, great care was taken to break the news to her as gently as possible. The news was that her husband was dead.

It was her sister Jo who told her. The news came in broken sentences, in hints. Her husband's friend Richards was there, too. It was he who had first learned. He had been in the newspaper office when the news came in. There had been a bad railroad wreck. Brently Mallard's name was on the list of "killed." Richards had only taken the time to check the name by telegram. Then he had hastened to the Mallard's home. He had wanted to beat any less careful, less tender friend in carrying the sad message.

She did not hear the story as many women have heard the same. She did not freeze up. She heard the words, and she knew all that they meant. She wept at once. She cried with sudden, wild abandonment in her sister's arms. Finally the storm of grief had spent itself. She went away to her room alone. She would have no one follow her.

There stood a comfortable, roomy armchair. Into this she sank. She felt pressed down by the tired feeling that haunted her body and seemed to reach into her soul.

The chair faced an open window. She could see the tops of trees, glowing with new spring life. The sweet breath of rain was in the air. Far, far off, someone was singing. The notes of the distant song reached her faintly. Countless birds were twittering here and there. There were patches of blue sky.

She sat with her head thrown back. She was quite still, except when a sob came up into her throat and shook her.

141

She was like a child who has cried itself to sleep and continues to sob in its dreams.

She was young, with a fair, clean-cut face. The few lines in it revealed repression as well as strength. But now there was a dull stare in her eyes. Their gaze was fixed away off on one of those patches of blue sky. It was not a thoughtful gaze. Rather, it showed that all thinking had stopped.

There was something new coming to her. She sat waiting for it, with fear. What was it? She did not know. It was too new, too strange to name. But she felt it, creeping out of the sky. It reached toward her through the sounds, the smells, the colors that filled the air.

Now her chest rose and fell rapidly. She was beginning to recognize this thing that was coming to possess her. She was trying to beat it back with her will. But her will was as powerless as her two slender hands would have been.

Suddenly she stopped fighting. She let herself go. And as she did so, a little whispered word came to her slightly parted lips. She said it over and over under her breath. "Free. Free. Free." The blank stare and the look of terror that had followed it went from her eyes. They stayed clear and bright. Her heart beat fast. The rushing blood warmed and relaxed every inch of her body.

Was it some monstrous joy that held her? She did not stop to ask. Somehow, she knew better. The suggestion was beside the point.

She knew that she would weep again. She would see his kind, tender hands folded in death. . . . The face that had never looked except with love upon her. . . . The face—fixed and gray and dead. But she saw beyond that bitter moment. The long line of years to come would belong to her. To *her!* *Only* to her! And she spread her arms out to them in welcome.

There would be no one to live *for* during those years.

She would live for herself. No powerful will would be bending her. . . . No blind effort with which men and women believe they have a right to force a private will upon another person. Yes, that was the thing! A kind intention or a cruel intention—it didn't matter. Forcing one's will upon another was still a crime. Or so it seemed to her in that brief moment of clear, bright thought.

And yet she had loved Brently Mallard—sometimes. Often she had not. What did it matter! Love was an unsolved mystery. What could it count for now? Something else was now possessing her. She suddenly knew it as the strongest force she had ever felt.

"Free! Body and soul free!" she kept whispering.

Jo, her sister, was now kneeling outside the closed door. Jo's lips were to the keyhole. "Louise, open the door! I beg you, please! Open the door. You'll make yourself sick. What are you doing, Louise? For heaven's sake open the door."

"Go away. I am not making myself sick." No; she was drinking in the very elixir of life through that window.

Her thoughts were running riot. They raced through the days ahead of her. Spring days. Summer days. All sorts of days that would be her own. She breathed a quick prayer that her life might be long.

She stood up finally. She opened the door to her sister's pleadings. There was a look of victory in her clear eyes. She clasped her sister's waist. Together they went down the stairs. Richards stood waiting for them at the bottom.

Someone was opening the front door with a key. It was Brently Mallard who entered. An unconcerned, very ordinary Brently Mallard. He stood there carrying suitcase and umbrella. He had been far from the scene of the accident. He did not even know there had been one. He looked amazed at Jo's piercing cry. Richards made a quick motion to hide him from his wife's eyes.

But Richards was too late.

Soon the doctors came. They said she had died of a heart attack—of joy that kills.

Recall

1. Richards learns of Brently Mallard's death (a) in a newspaper office (b) from an uncle (c) from the sister, Jo
2. After crying a while at the news, Louise Mallard (a) freezes up (b) tries to forget the whole thing (c) goes to her room to be alone
3. Louise tries to fight off the new feelings that come to possess her. Finally she (a) succeeds in fighting them off (b) accepts them as her true feelings (c) wishes for death as an escape
4. Jo's belief that Louise's brooding is making her sick is (a) correct (b) incorrect (c) a clever lie
5. There are two big surprises at the end of the story. The first is that (a) Richards is at the bottom of the stairs (b) Brently is alive (c) Louise dies

Infer

6. "The few lines in [her face] revealed repression as well as strength." One thing Louise Mallard had repressed had been her (a) great love for her husband (b) need to get a job (c) true feelings about her marriage
7. The story indicates that (a) some women feel put down by their husbands (b) everyone should get married someday (c) most marriages go bad

8. Louise refuses to ask if her new feeling is one of "monstrous joy." Nearest in meaning to *monstrous joy* is the term (a) *dangerous love* (b) *guilty happiness* (c) *animal-like pleasures*

9. Which statement is probably correct? (a) Louise Mallard's husband had been killed in an accident. (b) A man named Brently Mallard had been killed in a train wreck. (c) The railroad accident was made up by a newspaper writer.

10. In truth, Mrs. Mallard died of (a) joy that kills (b) illness (c) the shock of disappointment

Vocabulary Review

Write on your paper the word in *italics* that belongs in each blank. Use each word only once.

abandonment	*intention*	*piercing*	*will*
elixir	*monstrous*	*repression*	

1. Dancing with wild _____, few people in the disco saw the fire start.

2. People with lots of _____ power can force themselves to do, or not do, certain things.

3. Carmen never told Jamie how she felt about him, but the _____ of her feelings wasn't easy.

4. An evil, _____ thought forced itself into Brad's mind.

5. Was his _____ really to kill the cat?

6. Joe's loud, _____ cry saved him from the muggers.

7. Barb's always happy, as though she drinks daily of the _____ of life.

145

Critical Thinking

1. "The Story of an Hour" is well written. Look, for instance, at the very first paragraph. In just three sentences, the author sets up certain expectations (ideas about events to come) in the reader's mind. What does the first paragraph tell us might happen? How is this related to what does happen at the end of the story?

2. Now look at the end of the story. In just a few lines, a "dead" person comes back to life and a living person dies. The last four words are "— of joy that kills." These are the doctors' words. Do you think her husband would agree with them? Why, or why not?

3. Right after Louise enters her room, the author mentions things in the natural world outside the window—trees, birds, blue sky, etc. In such a short, tightly written story, these things must have a purpose. What is that purpose?

4. Louise's feelings, of course, come from the inside. But as she experiences them, they seem to come from the outside (". . . creeping out of the sky. It reached toward her. . . ."). Does this seem real to you? Have you ever experienced the same thing? If so, try to explain it.

5. "The Story of an Hour" is full of opposites: life—death, the inside—the outside, living for oneself—living for another, sadness—joy, repression—abandonment. One of these opposites is contained in the odd term "monstrous joy." Why is the term odd? What does it mean in the context or setting of the story?

6. This story shocked some readers in the 1890's. Explain why.

The Child Watcher

Ernest Harrison

*Titles can be teasers. Often they lead us to ask
questions. Just think of some of the titles you've met
in this book. What is an "Eye Catcher"? Why do
"Only the Guilty Run"? What happens "In a
Dim Room"?*

*What does "The Child Watcher" mean to you?
A child who watches? A person who watches a
child? This story will be more fun if you decide right
now.*

*The Reverend Ernest Harrison is a priest who
lives in Canada. Reading and writing short stories is
a hobby. It helps him take his mind off his more
serious duties.*

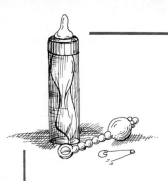

Vocabulary Preview

BLURRED (BLURD) not sharp and clear; fuzzy
• Idalie showed me a *blurred* photo of her boy friend.

CYNICAL (SIN i cul) doubting; holding a low opinion of human beings
• Mr. Rossi is *cynical* about politics and politicians. ⸳⸳

EXPRESSION (eks PRESH un) a look that shows feeling or meaning
• The *expression* on Dad's face meant "no."

IMPOSE (im POZE) to put or lay on something, as a tax
• The state is going to *impose* a tax on restaurant meals.

SHRIEK (SHREEK) a very loud scream
• He let out a *shriek* when he saw the mouse.

WOMB (WOOM) the "sack" that holds a baby before birth
• At birth, a baby passes from the mother's *womb* into the outside air.

ESTHER LOOKED DOWN AT THE BABY WITH interest. He lay in his crib, playing with his toes. His bright eyes were on one toe that stuck out at an odd angle. Suddenly he tired of his study. He turned over on his stomach. He tried to move himself to the corner of his crib.

Though unable to smile, Esther felt a warm glow within her body. A movement in her womb held out its happy promise. A flood of confused memories swept over her. Moments of joy. Moments of sadness. And now, the nearness of birth. These things could not be put into words, perhaps not even into thoughts. But the feelings ran strong in her. She looked down once more at the baby. Soon, the movement in her belly told her. Soon she———— Her thoughts broke off in a blurred picture she could not quite hold.

The baby made an awkward turn. His diaper pin popped open. A sharp point; a sharper pain. Now he was howling. The door opened within seconds. The anxious mother swept into the room.

"My baby, my precious little boy . . . Diddums cry for mummy?" She picked him up in her arms. She snuggled him to her. "Look, Esther, isn't he a *silly* little boy to cry like that? Why, when Esther is here?" A loud howl came as her hand pressed the pin into his skin again. With it, she discovered the cause of his complaint. All was apology. "Oh, so that's it! Did *nasty* mummy hurt her little darling? There, there . . ." The words ran on without end.

Esther felt slightly sick.

Her first pains came soon. And then, the joy of birth. It is easy to be cynical about the strength of mother love. But nature imposes it at the very moment that a life comes into the world. And in the same way, once the first sound of a new breathing comes, there is bitterness if the life is snatched away. . . .

It was later. Esther once more looked down at the baby. But now there was envy in her heart. His mother had patted and cuddled him, not knowing of Esther's troubled feelings. Now she had gone from the room. Esther remained to watch the child.

She gulped slightly. The memories of joy had faded. Dim thoughts tumbled through her mind. She recalled the pains clearly, and the cries of life. Then the joy, so quickly ended. She did not understand death. Or what made it different from life. Or what left sorrow in her heart. If the mother had thought of asking her, Esther would have remained dumb.

But she knew what hate was, and envy. The baby began to crow with pleasure. "Come," his look declared. "Don't be sad, Esther. I don't know what makes you so unhappy. But the world isn't worth it. You'll forget, all right, just as I do. See, I've got a great big foot to show you. . . . I know how mad mummy always makes you. She makes me mad, too. Sometimes, that is. Come *on,* Esther, snap out of it. Anyway, I love you, don't I? Now, doesn't that make it up to you?"

Esther looked at him without expression. He turned away to explore the pillow.

Without warning, the hate in her heart overflowed. She knew suddenly what she wanted to do. She turned her head toward the door, listening carefully. There was no sound.

She turned back to the baby, watching his actions. She was still not certain how she would do it. But she wanted to do it more than anything in the world.

The child's bottom stuck in the air. It moved from side to side as he tried to push his head through the crib rails.

Esther passed the tip of her tongue through her lips. She felt a tightness in her throat. She moved forward, then stopped. The baby found that his head was too large. He pulled away. He wriggled over onto his back.

He was about to put his feet up and touch them with his hands. But just then, his eyes caught Esther's expression. He raised his voice—a sudden, choking scream. Esther fell upon him. The cry rose to a shriek. Filled with hatred for the world, Esther tore madly at him.

The door banged open. The baby's mother rushed into the room. Esther whirled, now caught. But then she was struggling for her own life, being choked out of her by the woman who had drowned her newborn kittens.

Recall

1. In the first section of the story, Esther looks at the baby with (a) anger (b) interest (c) fierce hate
2. Esther is filled with feelings concerning (a) getting enough to eat (b) her love for the mother (c) giving birth herself

3. The baby starts to cry when it is (a) stuck with a diaper pin (b) picked up by Esther (c) unable to roll over
4. In the last section of the story, Esther looks at the baby with (a) love (b) amusement (c) hate and envy
5. The story ends with (a) the mother choking the baby (b) Esther choking the baby (c) the mother choking Esther

Infer

6. It is very important to the story that Esther never (a) washes herself (b) speaks (c) eats
7. Near the end of the story is the sentence, "But she [Esther] wanted to do it more than anything in the world." In this sentence the word *it* means (a) injure or kill the baby (b) help the mother (c) help the baby
8. The story makes us think *most* about (a) the shape of cribs (b) what babies would say if they could talk (c) the strength of mother love
9. Esther attacks the baby mainly to punish (a) herself (b) the mother (c) the baby
10. The important surprise in the story is an inference, since it's not stated directly. This is the fact that Esther (a) doesn't really exist (b) has strong feelings (c) is a cat

Vocabulary Review

1. If your teacher *imposes* some classroom rules, she or he (a) changes them (b) removes them (c) puts them into effect
2. A *cynical* person would probably not (a) like vegetables (b) trust many people (c) be a hard worker

152

3. A *blurred expression* is the same thing as (a) a fuzzy look (b) a pleased smile (c) an amusing way of saying something

4. A *womb* is a (a) Spanish house (b) small western animal (c) baby's home before birth

5. If a man *shrieked* in the street, he might be (a) humming old songs (b) frightened by something (c) smiling at some young lovers

Critical Thinking

1. In this story, the surprise isn't simply held till the ending. It's held till the *very last word.* Yet there are clues. The first clue comes at the beginning of paragraph two. What are some others? Find as many as you can.

2. What were your feelings when you finished the story? Most readers like the story. But one reader stated, "It left a bad taste in my mouth." What about you? Do you think the story's effect has anything to do with the reader's feelings about cats? Explain.

3. The author of the story tries to imagine what goes on inside an animal's head. Many writers, when they do this, go too far. They give animals thoughts and feelings that could only be human. In your opinion, does Ernest Harrison go too far? Is there anything about the cat Esther that you find hard to believe? Explain.

4. The author of "The Child Watcher" makes excellent use of *figurative language.* That is, he uses words for what they suggest, not for what they really mean. In each of the following sentences, explain what the term in *italics* really means. Then explain what it means in the context of the sentence.

Example: ". . . Esther felt a warm *glow* within her body."

Real meaning: a shining steady light
Meaning here: pleasant feeling

a) A movement in her womb *held out* its happy promise.
b) A *flood* of confused memories swept over her.
c) The anxious mother *swept* into the room.
d) The baby began to *crow* with pleasure.
e) Without warning, the hate in her heart *overflowed.*

Doctor's Orders

John F. Suter

*Here's a story you'll probably read twice. Not
because you'll have to. Because you'll want to.*

*Some stories are like that. When you begin
them, everything seems mixed up and confusing.
Then, little by little, you begin to fit the pieces
together. Finally, toward the end of the story, the
truth bursts across your brain. You sit there reeling.
You ask yourself, "Did the story really say that?
What I thought it said?" And zip— you're back
at the beginning, reading it again.*

*Read every word carefully. This skillful shocker
is worth the effort.*

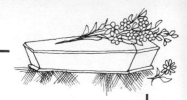

Vocabulary Preview

CONVINCE (kun VINS) to cause to believe; to make a person feel sure of something
  • Dorrie's quick answers *convince* me that she is telling the truth.

RESPONSIBILITY (ri SPON suh BIL uh tee) something a person is responsible for, or must care for
  • Mom says making my bed is my *responsibility* now.

SENSE (SENS) to feel, understand, be aware of
  • I could *sense* that Ed was nervous on the stage.

SENSIBLE (SEN suh bul) having good judgment
  • A *sensible* person is usually trusted by others.

THROB (THROB) to beat rapidly, especially with pain
  • The finger that the baseball hit will probably *throb* all afternoon.

WILL (WIL) a legal paper containing a person's wishes about who gets his or her property after death
  • Mr. Hart's *will* left his farm to his only child, Charlotte.

THE PAIN, THE PAIN IS EVERYWHERE. NO, not everywhere. But I throb in places where there is no real pain. And now it is only an ache and a tired feeling. It seems as if there is no time, no space, nothing but this. But I am a little stronger than I was. So little. But I *am* stronger. I have to get well. I intend to get well. I will get well.

"Mr. Shaw, I think she'll come out of it all right. As you know, it was either your wife or the baby, for a while. But she's improved, I know that. Of course, there will always be the weakness. We can't correct that."

"I understand. Just to have her well again is all I care about."

I had better open my eyes. Jeff isn't here. I can't sense him. But I can stand the white room now. I no longer have a wish to die. No, even though he didn't live. I could cry and cry about it. I wanted to when Jeff first told me. But there is no strength in those sorts of tears. I will get well.

"You did tell her that the baby died?"

"Yes, Doctor. It was hard for her to take at first. Very hard. Then I told her that it had been a boy. That pleased her, in spite of—of what happened."

There. The world is back. So much sunshine in the room. So many flowers. I wonder if Jeff——

"Did you tell her that the child is already buried?"

"Not yet. If you're sure that she's stronger, I'll tell her today."

"You don't think she'll hold it against you, Mr. Shaw? For going ahead with the funeral, I mean."

"Jessie is very level headed, Doctor. She'll understand that we couldn't wait. And—if you don't think it's out of style to say so—we love each other."

I'm sure Jeff has done whatever is best. If only it—he —had lived until I could have seen him. . . . How long have I been here? Where is Jeff? Is he being sensible, as I begged him to be? Is he at work? I hope so. The job is so important to him. Oh, I do love him! And I do so want to give him fine children.

"Perhaps, then, Mr. Shaw, it would be better for you to tell her the rest of it. Better, I mean, than for me to do it. It might be easier for her to believe someone who loves her. Sometimes people think they know more than doctors do."

"That part won't be easy."

I hope the children will look like Jeff. I'm not ugly. But I'm so—plain. Jeff has the looks for both of us. That's one of the reasons they all said he was only after my money. But he's refused to let me help him. He's independent. He keeps working hard managing the sporting-goods department. And why? He wants to support us. Neither of us would ever have to work again, if we didn't want to. I must get well, for his sake. I will get well.

"Easy or hard, Mr. Shaw, it has to be done. Someone has to tell her. It will come best from you. She must never try to have a child again. Never. It will kill her. Make no mistake about it—having another child will kill her."

"I'll take the responsibility, Doctor. You needn't say a thing to her. I think I can convince her. Perhaps I can even persuade her to move away for a while. A room's all set up for the baby. Those things shouldn't keep haunting her."

I'm glad I made my will before I came to the hospital. I'm glad I made it in Jeff's favor. He doesn't know about it. And it wasn't necessary, as it turned out. But I'm glad. He's been so good to me that now I'm sure of him. . . .

The door swung inward, silently. She turned her head, slowly. A tired smile crept across her white face. A tall young man with crinkled blond hair was in the doorway.

"Jeff."

He was at her bedside, kissing her hand. "Jessie."

When they both could speak, she gripped his fingers. "Jeff, I've been lying here thinking. Everybody has troubles of some kind or other. We can overcome this. I'm going to get strong, fast. Then we're going to have another baby. Just as quickly as we can. Aren't we?"

He smiled proudly. The truth was exactly the right answer.

"We certainly are, sweetheart. We certainly are."

Recall

1. Jessie has recently made a will in favor of (a) her child (b) the hospital (c) Jeff
2. In the conversations between Jeff and the doctor, we learn that (a) the child looked like Jessie (b) Jessie will be ill all her life (c) Jessie must not have another child
3. Jessie believes that Jeff (a) is only after her money (b) really doesn't want children (c) is a loving and honest person
4. At the end of the story, the plan to have another child is (a) shared by Jessie and Jeff (b) Jessie's only (c) Jeff's only
5. The story is organized in twelve short sections. Every other section contains (a) Jeff's thoughts (b) Jessie's thoughts (c) Jessie's spoken words

Infer

6. Just before the story begins, Jessie wished to die because she (a) knew she couldn't have another baby (b) thought she would be in pain all her life (c) had lost her baby
7. The time that passed between the baby's birth and the story itself was about three (a) hours (b) days (c) months
8. More than anything else, Jeff seems to love (a) Jessie (b) children (c) money
9. Jessie's trust in her husband is (a) a mistake (b) not complete (c) well deserved by Jeff
10. At the end of the story, Jeff is thinking of (a) the joys of another child (b) large hospital bills (c) a kind of murder

Vocabulary Review

1. If you are *convinced* of something, you (a) should find the person who took it (b) believe it to be true (c) might thank the person who forgave you
2. A *sensible* person would probably (a) be a good athlete (b) have an unusually good sense of hearing (c) keep out of trouble
3. If your *responsibility* is to make a *will,* you should see a (a) home repair expert (b) lawyer (c) religious leader
4. A heart that *throbs* (a) beats rapidly (b) is certainly weak (c) is always a sign of true love
5. Even in a dark, silent room, you can sometimes *sense* the presence of other people. In other words, you (a) can see them (b) avoid them (c) feel somehow that they are there

Critical Thinking

1. Near the end of the story is the sentence, "The truth was exactly the right answer." Explain the importance of this sentence in your own words. What "truth" is referred to? And from Jeff's point of view, why is it "the right answer"?
2. This "truth" at the end comes as a shock because Jeff has lied throughout the story. Find what you think is his biggest lie. Explain what the truth really is in that case.
3. Did you foresee the surprise ending? If so, what clues helped you? If not, look back for clues that might have helped.
4. Suppose Jeff goes ahead with his plan and a year later Jessie is dead. Would you use the word "murder" to describe his actions? Explain.

5. With its twelve short sections, the story is written in an unusual way. Explain why the author chose to tell the story in this way. What kinds of information does the reader need to know? Why would the regular method of telling a story be awkward in this case?

Sorry, Wrong Number

Lucille Fletcher

Mrs. Stevenson has a problem. She's an invalid. She's been in bed for years. One evening she picks up the telephone receiver to call her husband. But something goes wrong with the phone company's wires. She can't reach her husband. Instead, she hears two people planning a murder.

As you read "Sorry, Wrong Number," remember that Mrs. Stevenson is easily excited. She soon becomes unnerved—and you will too. Take a few deep breaths right now. Then turn the page and read one of the most thrilling radio plays ever written.

Vocabulary Preview

APPREHEND (ap ri HEND) seize; arrest
- The police could not *apprehend* the robbers.

CIVIC (SIV ik) having to do with good citizenship
- Voting in elections is a *civic* duty.

CLIENT (KLY unt) a person who pays for some duty performed
- The lawyer's *client* was found guilty.

COINCIDENCE (ko IN suh dense) things happening at the same time for no logical reason
- For mother and daughter to have the same birthday is a *coincidence.*

EXPLICITLY (eks PLIS it lee) very clearly
- The teacher gave the homework assignment *explicitly.*

PRECINCT (PREE singkt) a part of a city
- Each *precinct* has its own police station.

UNSPEAKABLY (un SPEEK uh blee) horribly; not to be spoken of
- Dom's behavior was *unspeakably* bad.

Act I

SOUND: *Number being dialed on phone; busy signal.*

MRS. STEVENSON *(a complaining, self-centered person):* Oh—*dear!* (*Slams down receiver. Dials* OPERATOR.)

OPERATOR: Your call, please?

MRS. STEVENSON: Operator? I've been dialing Murray Hill 4–0098 now for the last three quarters of an hour, and the line is always busy. But I don't see how it *could* be busy that long. Will you try it for me, please?

OPERATOR: Murray Hill 4–0098? One moment, please.

MRS. STEVENSON: I don't see how it could be busy all this time. It's my husband's office. He's working late tonight, and I'm all alone here in the house. My health is very poor—and I've been feeling so nervous all day—

OPERATOR: Ringing Murray Hill 4–0098.

(SOUND: *Phone buzz. It rings three times. Receiver is picked up at other end.*)

MAN: Hello.

MRS. STEVENSON: Hello? *(A little puzzled.)* Hello. Is Mr. Stevenson there?

MAN *(into phone, as though he had not heard):* Hello. *(Louder.)* Hello.

SECOND MAN *(slow, heavy voice, faintly foreign accent):* Hello.

FIRST MAN: Hello, George?

GEORGE: Yes, sir.

MRS. STEVENSON *(louder and more commanding, to phone):* Hello. Who's this? What number am I calling, please?

FIRST MAN: We have heard from our client. He says the coast is clear for tonight.

GEORGE: Yes, sir.

FIRST MAN: Where are you now?

GEORGE: In a phone booth.

FIRST MAN: Okay. You know the address. At eleven o'clock the private patrolman goes around to the bar on Second Avenue for a beer. Be sure that all the lights downstairs are out. There

165

should be only one light visible from the street. At eleven fifteen a subway train crosses the bridge. It makes a noise in case her ·window is open and she should scream.

MRS. STEVENSON *(shocked)*: Oh—*hello!* What number is this, please?

GEORGE: Okay. I understand.

FIRST MAN: Make it quick. As little blood as possible. Our client does not wish to make her suffer long.

GEORGE: A knife okay, sir?

FIRST MAN: Yes. A knife will be okay. And remember—remove the rings and bracelets, and the jewelry in the bureau drawer. Our client wishes it to look like simple robbery.

GEORGE: Okay, I get—

           (SOUND: *A soft buzzing signal.*)

MRS. STEVENSON *(clicking phone)*: Oh! *(Soft buzzing signal continues. She hangs up.)* How awful! How unspeakably—

           (SOUND: *Dialing. Phone buzz.*)

OPERATOR: Your call, please?

MRS. STEVENSON *(up-tight and breathless, into phone)*: Operator, I— I've just been cut off.

OPERATOR: I'm sorry, madam. What number were you calling?

MRS. STEVENSON: Why—it was supposed to be Murray Hill 4– 0098, but it wasn't. Some wires must have crossed—I was cut into a wrong number—and—I've just heard the most dreadful thing—a—a murder—and— *(As an order)* Operator, you'll simply have to retrace that call at once.

OPERATOR: I beg your pardon, madam—I don't quite—

MRS. STEVENSON: Oh—I know it was a wrong number, and I had no business listening—but these two men—they were cold-blooded fiends—and they were going to murder somebody— some poor innocent woman—who was all alone—in a house near a bridge. And we've got to stop them—we've got to—

OPERATOR *(patiently)*: What number were you calling, madam?

MRS. STEVENSON: That doesn't matter. This was a *wrong* number. And *you* dialed it. And we've got to find out what it was— immediately!

OPERATOR: But—madam—

MRS. STEVENSON: Oh, why are you so stupid? Look, it was obviously a case of some little slip of the finger. I told you to try

Murray Hill 4–0098 for me—you dialed it—but your finger must have slipped—and I was connected with some other number—and I could hear them, but they couldn't hear me. Now, I simply fail to see why you couldn't make that same mistake again—on purpose—why you couldn't *try* to dial Murray Hill 4–0098 in the same careless sort of way—

OPERATOR *(quickly)*: Murray Hill 4–0098? I will try to get it for you, madam.

MRS. STEVENSON: *Thank* you.

(Sound of ringing; busy signal.)

OPERATOR: I am sorry. Murray Hill 4–0098 is busy.

MRS. STEVENSON *(madly clicking receiver)*: Operator. Operator.

OPERATOR: Yes, madam.

MRS. STEVENSON *(angrily)*: You *didn't* try to get that wrong number at all. I asked explicitly. And all you did was dial correctly.

OPERATOR: I am sorry. What number were you calling?

MRS. STEVENSON: Can't you, for once, forget what number I was calling, and do something specific? Now I want to trace that call. It's my civic duty—it's *your* civic duty—to trace that call—and to apprehend those dangerous killers—and if *you* won't—

OPERATOR: I will connect you with the Chief Operator.

MRS. STEVENSON: *Please!*

(Sound of ringing.)

CHIEF OPERATOR *(A cool pro)*: This is the Chief Operator.

MRS. STEVENSON: Chief Operator? I want you to trace a call. A telephone call. Immediately. I don't know where it came from, or who was making it, but it's absolutely necessary that it be tracked down. Because it was about a murder. Yes, a terrible, cold-blooded murder of a poor innocent woman—tonight—at eleven fifteen.

CHIEF OPERATOR: I see.

MRS. STEVENSON *(high-strung, demanding)*: Can you trace it for me? Can you track down those men?

CHIEF OPERATOR: It depends, madam.

MRS. STEVENSON: Depends on what?

CHIEF OPERATOR: It depends on whether the call is still going on. If it's a live call, we can trace it on the equipment. If it's been disconnected, we can't.

MRS. STEVENSON: Disconnected?

CHIEF OPERATOR: If the parties have stopped talking to each other.

MRS. STEVENSON: Oh—but—but of course they must have stopped talking to each other by *now.* That was at least five minutes ago—and they didn't sound like the type who would make a long call.

CHIEF OPERATOR· Well, I can try tracing it. Now—what is your name, madam?

MRS. STEVENSON: Mrs. Stevenson. Mrs. Elbert Stevenson. But—listen—

CHIEF OPERATOR *(writing it down):* And your telephone number?

MRS. STEVENSON *(more bothered):* Plaza 4–2295. But if you go on wasting all this time—

CHIEF OPERATOR: And what is your reason for wanting this call traced?

MRS. STEVENSON: My reason? Well—for heaven's sake—isn't it obvious? I overhear two men—they're killers—they're planning to murder this woman—it's a matter for the police.

CHIEF OPERATOR: Have you told the police?

MRS. STEVENSON: No. How could I?

CHIEF OPERATOR: You're making this check into a private call purely as a private individual?

MRS. STEVENSON: Yes. But meanwhile—

CHIEF OPERATOR: Well, Mrs. Stevenson—I seriously doubt whether we could make this check for you at this time just on your say-so as a private individual. We'd have to have something more official.

MRS. STEVENSON: Oh, for heaven's sake! You mean to tell me I can't report a murder without getting tied up in all this red tape? Why, it's perfectly idiotic. All right, then. I *will* call the police. *(She slams down receiver.)* Ridiculous!

(Sound of dialing.)

SECOND OPERATOR: Your call, please?

MRS. STEVENSON *(very annoyed):* The Police Department—*please.*

SECOND OPERATOR: Ringing the Police Department.

(Rings twice. Phone is picked up.)

SERGEANT DUFFY: Police Department. Precinct 43. Duffy speaking.

MRS. STEVENSON: Police Department? Oh. This is Mrs. Stevenson

—Mrs. Elbert Smythe Stevenson of 53 North Sutton Place. I'm calling up to report a murder.

DUFFY: Eh?

MRS. STEVENSON: I mean—the murder hasn't been committed yet. I just overheard plans for it over the telephone . . . over a wrong number that the operator gave me. I've been trying to trace down the call myself, but everybody is so stupid—and I guess in the end you're the only people who could *do* anything.

DUFFY *(not too impressed):* Yes, ma'am.

MRS. STEVENSON *(trying to impress him):* It was a perfectly *definite* murder. I heard their plans distinctly. Two men were talking, and they were going to murder some woman at eleven fifteen tonight—she lived in a house near a bridge.

DUFFY: Yes, ma'am.

MRS. STEVENSON: And there was a private patrolman on the street. He was going to go around for a beer on Second Avenue. And there was some third man—a client—who was paying to have this poor woman murdered— They were going to take her rings and bracelets—and use a knife— Well, it's unnerved me dreadfully—and I'm not well—

DUFFY: I see. When was all this, ma'am?

MRS. STEVENSON: About eight minutes ago. Oh . . . *(relieved)* then you *can* do something? You *do* understand—

DUFFY: And what is your name, ma'am?

MRS. STEVENSON *(losing patience):* Mrs. Stevenson. Mrs. Elbert Stevenson.

DUFFY: And your address?

MRS. STEVENSON: 53 North Sutton Place. *That's* near a bridge, the Queensborough Bridge, you know—and *we* have a private patrolman on *our* street—and Second Avenue—

DUFFY: And what was that number you were calling?

MRS. STEVENSON: Murray Hill 4–0098. But—that wasn't the number I overheard. I mean Murray Hill 4–0098 is my husband's office. He's working late tonight, and I was trying to reach him to ask him to come home. I'm an invalid, you know—and it's the maid's night off—and I *hate* to be alone—even though he says I'm perfectly safe as long as I have the telephone right beside my bed.

DUFFY *(trying to end it):* Well, we'll look into it, Mrs. Stevenson, and see if we can check it with the telephone company.

MRS. STEVENSON *(using more patience):* But the telephone company said they couldn't check the call if the parties had stopped talking. I've already taken care of *that.*

DUFFY: Oh, yes?

MRS. STEVENSON *(getting bossy):* Personally I feel you ought to do something far more immediate and drastic than just check the call. What good does checking the call do, if they've stopped talking? By the time you track it down, they'll already have committed the murder.

DUFFY: Well, we'll take care of it, lady. Don't worry.

MRS. STEVENSON: I'd say the whole thing calls for a search—a complete and thorough search of the whole city. I'm very near a bridge, and I'm not far from Second Avenue. And I know *I'd* feel a whole lot better if you sent around a radio car to *this* neighborhood at once.

DUFFY: And what makes you think the murder's going to be committed in your neighborhood, ma'am?

MRS. STEVENSON: Oh, I don't know. The coincidence is so horrible. Second Avenue—the patrolman—the bridge—

DUFFY: Second Avenue is a very long street, ma'am. And do you happen to know how many bridges there are in the city of New York alone? Not to mention Brooklyn, Staten Island, Queens, and the Bronx? And how do you know there isn't some little house out on Staten Island—on some little Second Avenue you've never heard about? How do you know they were even talking about New York at all?

MRS. STEVENSON: But I heard the call on the New York dialing system.

DUFFY: How do you know it wasn't a long-distance call you overheard? Telephones are funny things. Look, lady, why don't you look at it this way? Supposing you hadn't broken in on that telephone call? Supposing you'd got your husband the way you always do? Would this murder have made any difference to you then?

MRS. STEVENSON: I suppose not. But it's so inhuman—so cold-blooded—

DUFFY: A lot of murders are committed in this city every day, ma'am. If we could do something to stop 'em, we would. But a clue of this kind that's so vague isn't much more use to us than no clue at all.

MRS. STEVENSON: But surely—

DUFFY: Unless, of course, you have some reason for thinking this call is phony—and that someone may be planning to murder *you?*

MRS. STEVENSON: *Me?* Oh, no, I hardly think so. I—I mean—why should anybody? I'm alone all day and night—I see nobody except my maid Eloise—she's a big two-hundred-pounder— she's too lazy to bring up my breakfast tray—and the only other person is my husband Elbert—he's crazy about me—adores me —waits on me hand and foot—he's scarcely left my side since I took sick twelve years ago—

DUFFY: Well, then, there's nothing for you to worry about, is there? And now, if you'll just leave the rest of this to us—

MRS. STEVENSON: But what will you *do?* It's so late—it's nearly eleven o'clock.

DUFFY *(firmly):* We'll take care of it, lady.

MRS. STEVENSON: Will you broadcast it all over the city? And send out squads? And warn your radio cars to watch out—especially in suspicious neighborhoods like mine?

DUFFY *(more firmly):* Lady, I *said* we'd take care of it. Just now I've got a couple of other matters here on my desk that require my immediate—

MRS. STEVENSON: Oh! *(She slams down receiver hard.)* Idiot. *(Looking at phone nervously.)* Now, why did I do that? Now he'll think I *am* a fool. Oh, why doesn't Elbert come home? *Why* doesn't he? *(Sound of dialing operator.)*

Vocabulary Preview

CATECHIZING (KAT uh KY zing) asking many questions
* I knew there'd be a lot of *catechizing* if I got home late.

ENTITLED (en TY tld) given or claimed as a right
* All children are *entitled* to a good education.

EXCLUSIVE (eks KLU siv) shutting out all or most persons
* Heidi went to an *exclusive* private school.

EXTENSION (eks TEN shun) a phone on the same line as another
* Mom had an *extension* put next to her bed.

INEFFICIENT (in uh FISH unt) not efficient; wasteful; poorly run
* England has many *inefficient* old factories.

REGISTERED (REJ is turd) listed; approved
* The *registered* nurse was a *registered* voter.

REGISTRY (REJ is tree) a list of registered persons
* Call the Nurses' *Registry* at the hospital if you want a nurse.

Act II

(*Sound of dialing operator.*)

OPERATOR: Your call, please?

MRS. STEVENSON: Operator, for heaven's sake, will you ring that Murray Hill 4–0098 number again? I can't think what's keeping him so long.

OPERATOR: Ringing Murray Hill 4–0098. *(Rings. Busy signal.)* The line is busy. Shall I—

MRS. STEVENSON *(nastily):* I can hear it. You don't have to tell me. I know it's busy. *(Slams down receiver.)* If I could only get out of this bed for a little while. If I could get a breath of fresh air— or just lean out the window—and see the street— *(The phone rings. She answers it instantly.)* Hello. Elbert? Hello. Hello. Hello. Oh, what's the *matter* with this phone? *Hello? Hello? (Slams down receiver.) (The phone rings again, once. She picks it up.)* Hello? Hello —Oh, for heaven's sake, who *is* this? Hello, Hello, *Hello. (Slams down receiver. Dials operator.)*

THIRD OPERATOR: Your call, please?

MRS. STEVENSON *(very annoyed and commanding):* Hello, operator. I don't know what's the matter with this telephone tonight, but it's positively driving me crazy. I've never seen such inefficient, miserable service. Now, look. I'm an invalid, and I'm very nervous, and I'm *not* supposed to be annoyed. But if this keeps on much longer—

THIRD OPERATOR *(a young, sweet type):* What seems to be the trouble, madam?

MRS. STEVENSON: Well, everything's wrong. The whole world could be murdered, for all you people care. And now, my phone keeps ringing—

OPERATOR: Yes, madam?

MRS. STEVENSON: Ringing and ringing and ringing every five seconds or so, and when I pick it up, there's no one there.

OPERATOR: I am sorry, madam. If you will hang up, I will test it for you.

MRS. STEVENSON: I don't want you to test it for me. I want you to put through that call—whatever it is—at once.

OPERATOR *(gently):* I am afraid that is not possible, madam.

MRS. STEVENSON *(storming):* Not possible? And why may I ask?

OPERATOR: The system is automatic, madam. If someone is trying to dial your number, there is no way to check whether the call is coming through the system or not—unless the person who is trying to reach you complains to his particular operator—

MRS. STEVENSON: Well, of all the stupid, complicated—! And meanwhile *I've* got to sit here in my bed, *suffering* every time that phone rings, imagining everything—

OPERATOR: I will try to check it for you, madam.

MRS. STEVENSON: Check it! Check it! That's all anybody can do. Of all the stupid, idiotic . . .! *(She hangs up.)*. Oh—what's the use . . . *(Instantly* MRS. STEVENSON'S *phone rings again. She picks up the receiver. Wildly.)* Hello. HELLO. Stop ringing, do you hear me? Answer me? What do you want? Do you realize you're driving me crazy? Stark, staring—

MAN *(dull, flat voice):* Hello. Is this Plaza 4–2295?

MRS. STEVENSON *(catching her breath):* Yes. Yes. This is Plaza 4–2295.

MAN: This is Western Union. I have a telegram here for Mrs. Elbert Stevenson. Is there anyone there to receive the message?

MRS. STEVENSON *(trying to calm herself):* I am Mrs. Stevenson.

WESTERN UNION *(reading flatly):* The telegram is as follows: "Mrs. Elbert Stevenson. 53 North Sutton Place, New York, New York. Darling. Terribly sorry. Tried to get you for last hour, but line busy. Leaving for Boston 11 P.M. tonight on urgent business. Back tomorrow afternoon. Keep happy. Love. Signed. Elbert."

MRS. STEVENSON *(shocked, to herself):* Oh—no—

WESTERN UNION: That is all, madam. Do you wish us to deliver a copy of the message?

MRS. STEVENSON: No—no, thank you.

WESTERN UNION: Thank you, madam. Good night. *(He hangs up phone.)*

MRS. STEVENSON *(softly, to phone):* Good night. *(She hangs up slowly, suddenly bursting into tears.)* No—no—it isn't true! He couldn't do it. Not when he knows I'll be all alone. It's some trick—some fiendish— *(She dials operator.)*

OPERATOR *(coolly):* Your call, please?

MRS. STEVENSON: Operator—try that Murray Hill 4–0098 number for me just once more, please.

OPERATOR: Ringing Murray Hill 4–0098. *(Call goes through. We hear ringing at other end. Ring after ring.)*

MRS. STEVENSON: He's gone. Oh, Elbert, how could you? How could you—? *(She hangs up phone, sobbing with pity to herself, turning nervously.)* But I can't be alone tonight. I can't. If I'm alone one more second— I don't care what he says—or what the expense is—I'm a sick woman—I'm entitled— *(She dials* INFOR-MATION.*)*

INFORMATION: This is Information.

MRS. STEVENSON: I want the telephone number of Henchley Hospital.

INFORMATION: Henchley Hospital? Do you have the address, madam?

MRS. STEVENSON: No. It's somewhere in the seventies, though. It's a very small, private, and exclusive hospital where I had my appendix out two years ago. Henchley. *H-E-N-C—*

INFORMATION: One moment, please.

MRS. STEVENSON: Please—hurry. And please—what *is* the time?

INFORMATION: I do not know, madam. You may find out the time by dialing Meridian 7–1212.

MRS. STEVENSON *(angered):* Oh, for heaven's sake! Couldn't you—?

INFORMATION: The number of Henchley Hospital is Butterfield 7–0105, madam.

MRS. STEVENSON: Butterfield 7–0105. *(She hangs up before she finishes speaking, and immediately dials number as she repeats it.)*
(Phone rings.)

WOMAN *(middle-aged, solid, firm, practical):* Henchley Hospital, good evening.

MRS. STEVENSON: Nurses' Registry.

WOMAN: Who was it you wished to speak to, please?

MRS. STEVENSON *(bossy):* I want the Nurses' Registry at once. I want a trained nurse. I want to hire her immediately. For the night.

WOMAN: I see. And what is the nature of the case, madam?

175

MRS. STEVENSON: Nerves. I'm very nervous. I need soothing—and companionship. My husband is away—and I'm—

WOMAN: Have you been recommended to us by any doctor in particular, madam?

MRS. STEVENSON: No. But I really don't see why all this catechizing is necessary. I want a trained nurse. I was a patient in your hospital two years ago. And after all, I *do* expect to *pay* this person—

WOMAN: We quite understand that, madam. But registered nurses are very scarce just now—and our superintendent has asked us to send people out only on cases where the physician in charge feels it is absolutely necessary.

MRS. STEVENSON *(growing very upset):* Well, it *is* absolutely necessary. I'm a sick woman. I—I'm very upset. Very. I'm alone in this house—and I'm an invalid—and tonight I overheard a telephone conversation that upset me dreadfully. About a murder—a poor woman who was going to be murdered at eleven fifteen tonight —in fact, if someone doesn't come at once—I'm afraid I'll go out of my mind— *(Almost off handle by now.)*

WOMAN *(calmly):* I see. Well, I'll speak to Miss Phillips as soon as she comes in. And what is your name, madam?

MRS. STEVENSON: Miss Phillips. And when do you expect her in?

WOMAN: I really don't know, madam. She went out to supper at eleven o'clock.

MRS. STEVENSON: Eleven o'clock. But it's not eleven yet. *(She cries out.)* Oh, my clock *has* stopped. I thought it was running down. What time is it?

WOMAN: Just fourteen minutes past eleven.

(Sound of phone receiver being lifted on same line as MRS. STEVENSON'S. *A click.)*

MRS. STEVENSON *(crying out):* What's *that?*

WOMAN: What was what, madam?

MRS. STEVENSON: That—that click just now—in my own telephone? As though someone had lifted the receiver off the hook of the extension phone downstairs—

WOMAN I didn't hear it, madam. Now—about this—

MRS. STEVENSON *(scared):* But *I* did. There's someone in this house. Someone downstairs in the kitchen. And they're listening to me now. They're— *(Hangs up phone. In a hushed voice.)* I won't pick it up. I won't let them hear me. I'll be quiet—and they'll think— *(With growing terror.)* But if I don't call someone now—while they're still down there—there'll be no time. *(She picks up receiver. Soft buzzing signal. She dials operator. Ring twice.)*

OPERATOR *(a slow, lazy voice):* Your call, please?

MRS. STEVENSON *(a desperate whisper):* Operator, I—I'm in desperate trouble—I—

OPERATOR: I cannot hear you, madam. Please speak louder.

MRS. STEVENSON *(still whispering):* I don't dare. I—there's someone listening. Can you hear me now?

OPERATOR: Your call, please? What number are you calling, madam?

MRS. STEVENSON *(desperately):* You've got to hear me. Oh, please. You've got to help me. There's someone in this house. Someone who's going to murder me. And you've got to get in touch with the— *(Click of receiver being put down in* MRS. STEVENSON'S *home. Bursting out wildly.)* Oh, there it is—he's put it down—he's put down the extension—he's coming— *(She screams.)* He's coming up the stairs—*(Wildly.)* Give me the Police Department— *(Screaming.)* The police!

OPERATOR: Ringing the Police Department.

(Phone is rung. We hear sound of a subway train coming nearer. On second ring, MRS. STEVENSON *screams again, but roaring of train drowns out her voice. For a few seconds we hear nothing but roaring of train, then dying away, phone at police headquarters ringing.)*

DUFFY: Police Department. Precinct 43. Duffy speaking. *(Pause.)* Police Department. Duffy speaking.

GEORGE: Sorry. Wrong number. *(Hangs up.)*

Recall

1. As the play opens, Mrs. Stevenson has been (a) taking a nap (b) dialing her husband's office (c) worrying about her husband's safety

2. The murder that she hears being planned is supposed to (a) require a gun (b) take place the next day (c) look like a robbery

3. During most of the play, Mrs. Stevenson is (a) alone in her home (b) alone except for the maid (c) alone except for a criminal

4. Mrs. Stevenson becomes angry when the operator (a) calls her names (b) hangs up on her (c) can't dial a wrong number on purpose.

5. The chief operator tells Mrs. Stevenson that (a) all phone calls are recorded (b) a private individual can't have a call traced (c) criminals seldom risk using phones

6. Sergeant Duffy asks Mrs. Stevenson if she thinks *she* is going to be murdered. Mrs. Stevenson's reply is (a) *yes* (b) *maybe* (c) *no*

7. Sergeant Duffy repeatedly (a) thanks Mrs. Stevenson for the information (b) says "We'll take care of it, lady" (c) explains his plan to catch the criminals

8. Mrs. Stevenson believes that her husband (a) adores her (b) often tells her lies (c) is not really in his office

9. After she talks to Sergeant Duffy, Mrs. Stevenson's phone rings several times. This bothers her because (a) she hears only loud breathing (b) the police keep calling her (c) nobody's there when she answers the phone

10. A telegram informs Mrs. Stevenson that her husband (a) is leaving for Boston (b) will be home by midnight (c) has an out-of-order phone in his office

11. Toward the end of the play, Mrs. Stevenson (a) calls her maid Eloise (b) takes a sleeping pill (c) tries to get a nurse to care for her

12. Mrs. Stevenson knows she's not alone in the house when she hears (a) the door opening (b) a click on the phone (c) a gun being loaded

178

13. Mrs. Stevenson's last scream is drowned out by (a) the telephone ringing (b) Sergeant Duffy's voice (c) the roar of a subway train

14. The play takes place in (a) New York (b) Chicago (c) an unnamed city

15. Never in the play do we hear the voice of (a) a killer (b) a person trying to be helpful (c) Mr. Stevenson

Infer

16. Mrs. Stevenson seems to have plenty of (a) patience (b) money (c) friends

17. After talking to Mrs. Stevenson on the phone, Sergeant Duffy probably (a) does little or nothing about her complaint (b) sends a police officer to her home (c) sends a radio alarm all over the city

18. The "client" who paid for the criminal act was probably (a) George (b) Mr. Stevenson (c) a person not mentioned in the play

19. It's quite clear that at the end of the play (a) Mrs. Stevenson faints (b) Mrs. Stevenson is killed by George (c) the operator dials a wrong number by mistake

20. At the end of the play, Mr. Stevenson is probably (a) in his office (b) in his own home (c) traveling to Boston

Vocabulary Review

1. Houses in an *exclusive precinct* of a city would probably (a) be owned by police officers (b) cost a lot of money (c) be in need of repair

2. Some high schools offer a course called "civics." Such a course would deal with (a) nursing as a career (b) modern science (c) a citizen's duties and the government

3. Service at a certain garage might be called *unspeakably inefficient.* In other words, it is (a) horribly bad (b) silent but good (c) much too expensive

4. A *registry* of voters would be a (a) protest from many citizens (b) list of people registered to vote (c) person who registers citizens to vote

5. If you got the same mark on five spelling tests in a row, it would be (a) a *coincidence* (b) an *extension* (c) a *client*

6. "Beginning Monday, August 24, all senior clerks will be *entitled* to *extensions.*" In other words, they will (a) be given vacations (b) be given free books (c) have the right to desk phones

7. If you accuse a person of *catechizing* you, you're saying he or she is (a) stealing from you (b) asking too many questions (c) trying to shut you out of a group

8. A doctor's *client* would be (a) a patient (b) the person who prepares his income tax (c) a nurse

9. Let's hope you're never (a) *apprehended* (b) *entitled* (c) *registered*

10. A person who speaks *explicitly* speaks (a) softly (b) with a foreign accent (c) very clearly

Critical Thinking

1. Some readers of the play have called Mrs. Stevenson a "useless" person. In a way, this is correct. She's selfish and demanding. She doesn't even know how her own husband feels about her. But she does try to do one good thing in the play. What is it?

2. Early in the play, George is said to have a "faintly foreign accent." Why did the author bother to include this detail?

3. "Sorry, Wrong Number" makes excellent use of *irony.* That is, the reader (or listener) knows something that the main character does not know. When did you first think that Mrs. Stevenson herself might be murdered? (Look back.) When were you sure?

4. First and foremost, "Sorry, Wrong Number" was written as a thriller. But might the author be saying something serious between the lines? What is true of most of the people to whom Mrs. Stevenson talks? Does the play suggest anything about how people relate to each other in modern society?

5. Why is "Sorry, Wrong Number" a particularly good play for *radio?* It was an instant hit. Later, as you may know, it was turned into a popular movie. What kinds of things could the writer of a movie add to the original play? What kinds of things would *you* add?

Acknowledgments

We thank the following authors and companies for their permission to use copyrighted material:

CHATHAM PRESS, INC.—for "Captain Chase," "Frozen Citizens," and "The Ghastly Leg" by Mary Bolté, from *Haunted New England.* Copyright © MCMLXXII by Mary Bolté. Permission to reprint granted by The Chatham Press, Old Greenwich, Conn. 06870.

DRAMATISTS PLAY SERVICE, INC.—for "Sorry, Wrong Number" by Lucille Fletcher. Copyright © 1952, 1948 by Lucille Fletcher. Reprinted by permission of the Dramatists Play Service, Inc. and the author. Caution: "Sorry, Wrong Number" being duly copyrighted, is subject to a royalty. The amateur acting rights are controlled exclusively by the Dramatists Play Service, Inc., 440 Park Avenue South, New York, N.Y. 10016. No amateur production of the play may be given without obtaining in advance the written permission of the Dramatists Play Service, Inc. and paying the requisite fee.

ERNEST W. HARRISON—for "The Child Watcher" by Ernest W. Harrison. Copyright © 1958 by Davis Publications, Inc.; first published in *Ellery Queen's Mystery Magazine.*

HOUGHTON MIFFLIN COMPANY—for "The Mansion of the Dead." Adapted from "The Mansion of the Dead," *The Haunting of America* by Jean Anderson. Copyright © 1973 by Helen Jean Anderson. Used by permission of the publisher, Houghton Mifflin Company.

FREDERICK LAING—for "The Eye Catcher" (original title, "The Beau Catcher") by Frederick Laing. Adapted from a story by Frederick Laing, first published in *Collier's.* Copyright by Frederick Laing, 1971.

McINTOSH AND OTIS, INC.—for "Only the Guilty Run" by Vin Packer. Copyright © 1955 by Mercury Publications, Inc. Copyright assigned to Vin Packer, 1978. First published in *Ellery Queen's Mystery Magazine.* Reprinted by permission of McIntosh and Otis, Inc.

SCOTT MEREDITH LITERARY AGENCY, INC.—for "In a Dim Room" by Lord Dunsany, from *The Fourth Book of Jorkens,* Copyright © 1948, by Lord Dunsany. Reprinted by permission of the author's Estate and Scott Meredith Literary Agency, Inc., 845 Third Avenue, New York, N.Y. 10022.—for "The House" by André Maurois, from *The Collected Stories of André Maurois,* trans. by Adrienne Foulke. Copyright © 1967 by Washington Square Press, Inc. Reprinted by permission of the author and the author's agents, Scott Meredith Literary Agency, Inc., 845 Third Avenue, New York, N.Y. 10022.

JOHN F. SUTER—for "Doctor's Orders" by John F. Suter. Copyright © 1959 by Davis Publications, Inc.; first published in *Ellery Queen's Mystery Magazine.*